Robert Alan Mowbray Stevenson

**Peter Paul Rubens**

Robert Alan Mowbray Stevenson

**Peter Paul Rubens**

ISBN/EAN: 9783337226367

Printed in Europe, USA, Canada, Australia, Japan

Cover: Foto ©Raphael Reischuk / pixelio.de

More available books at **www.hansebooks.com**

# PETER PAUL RUBENS

*By*

## R. A. M. STEVENSON

*Author of "The Art of Velazquez," etc.*

LONDON

SEELEY AND CO., LIMITED, GREAT RUSSELL STREET

NEW YORK: THE MACMILLAN COMPANY

1898

# LIST OF ILLUSTRATIONS

## PLATES

## ILLUSTRATIONS PRINTED IN SEPIA

## ILLUSTRATIONS IN THE TEXT

# PETER PAUL RUBENS

## INTRODUCTION

*On the Appreciation and the Study of Rubens*

THOSE persons who are disquieted about the bearing of art upon morals turn round Rubens like a sanitary inspector sniffing about the apertures of a suspicious system of drainage. Immediately after the painter's death the moral character of his work was impugned, not by those princes of the church and the world who had been his patrons, but by the plump female burgess who had been his wife. Helen Fourment shuddered at the voluptuousness of his nymphs and goddesses; she would have destroyed several pictures, and one in particular, save for the amount of money offered for it by the Duke of Richelieu. Money avails much in a question of morals, as much with this kind of lady as fashion with one of a higher or gayer position. That aspect of the morals which looks askance at the nude is too trivial and too temporary a manifestation of human activity to occupy people who keep their eye on art from Assyria and Egypt onwards. A second view of the question has been held by Ruskin and by those who get all their views of painting from the study and practice of literature. According to them, the moral tone of the painter must be considered the main cause of his work, and painting should be a method of preaching which should be prefaced with prayer. A third set of people when they talk of the influence of morals on the painter mean temperament, which certainly counts for much both in morals and in art. This is only to say that all human activities, artistic or non-artistic, interested or disinterested, have their roots in the same life.

I distinguish between the effect of temperament and the effect of moral considerations upon a man. One is æsthetic; the other is not. Most men, I think, in no way conceive of moral judgments as feelings of æsthetic disgust or delight in actions, but rather regard them as restraints imposed by reason on these very feelings in the interests of the community. In real life, the man who has no interest in problems of conduct is stupidly dense to his surroundings. In the world of fiction, conduct affects the drama of life, affects its language, and so affects all the subjects of a poet or playwright. Even the most artificial and transient of these social regulations of conduct interest the writer : they form the bulk of the motifs of light reading. But they cannot easily supply direct motifs for the figure painter, still less for the landscape artist. On the other hand, if they offer no subjects to the painter, I cannot see that rules of self-mortification greatly influence the artistic temperament one way or the other. Restraint baulks the temperament that leads to direct and passionate acts in life, but it very little affects the feelings to which one gives expression in art. In fact, people should not closely consult men's lives for the reasons of their artistic performances ; the man of genius speaks of feelings that, whatever they may be, have been always suppressed by the world.

But it is through his temperament that the artist works; and since temperament is an influence in moral decisions, there may be a sort of second cousinship twice removed between paint and morals. Temperament works upon the landscape painter as effectively as upon the figure man ; it can turn him to large forms, to savage colour, or to peddling minuteness of pattern, and glassy smoothness of pigment ; just as it turns a figure painter to broad fleshy types, or to sharp bony models that show their anatomical structure.

Temperament directed Rubens in the choice of his types, and it is in reality colder temperaments, not stricter moralists, that have turned against his work. Patronised by princes and churchmen in his day, a favourite of fashion in our own country till the end of the first half of this century, Rubens has proved a stumbling-block to the modern Purists and Æsthetes, who can scarcely hear his name without agitation. Twenty years ago, when I confessed my admiration at Rubens's Medicis pictures I was looked upon by a circle of Purists as a person who had just committed an act of public indecency. " Oh those horrible fat women," say all who confuse art and nature, who cannot separate the contemplation of beauty from the animal distaste or desire of possession. When asked to look at Rubens's pictures one is not asked to fall on the necks of his models any more than one is required to feel bloodthirsty when looking at a battle-piece. Anything strong and consistent in character may be fit for a scheme of formal art ; for the working out of a pattern. And when we deal with impressionistic art, who shall say what is an unfit motif ? Light may break into delicious radiance upon corruption or ordure. In your real life you may refuse the society of people who are not thin, tall, willowy, virginal and built in clean, flat planes of bone and hard flesh ; yet in the imagined world of art you may allow Rubens to open the door upon a bevy of rich beauties that offer to the flood of warm light succulent forms, ample shapes, curved, coloured and creamy surfaces. So you may hate to wet your feet in dew and yet delight in the long grass of a *Morning* by Corot.

Neither in his art nor in his life is there any real ground to reproach Rubens with conventional immorality ; but against the refinement of his taste and the force of his imagination it is argued that he married two baggy women and could not forget them in his painting. These critics should remember that his tastes and his art, if not his culture, were all of a piece and natural to his temperament. In this century people condemn a man because his art is indifferent to his taste as a man ; because, in a word, he loves art for art's sake ; yet with the same breath almost they condemn the man whose art was the expression of his life. How would meagre forms have suited that broad flowing brush ? To Rubens, the husband of Helen Fourment, flesh was enticing in its largeness, its soft luminosity, its creamy evenness of tint, and he painted it with more sense of joy, and, as far as colour is concerned, with more insight than any other man.

In addition to fastidious niceties of morals and taste, a third impediment to the study and appreciation of Rubens arises from the nature, the quantity, and the distribution of his productions. He did not paint the greater part of the pictures issued from his studio that now people

the galleries of the world.    Great men clamoured for his works, and
he was content to superintend a school and to issue pictures that he had
merely designed or barely retouched.    It is a very different condition
of production from that of the present day, from that indeed of
Velazquez and of most later artists.    Rubens stands between the old
and the new.    He was a master decorator of churches, palaces, and town
halls; when he undertook a job he found workmen trained in his own
principles, started them by drawings, and at the end he gave their work
a few finishing brush strokes.    The system supported a good general
level of work, diminished the output of bad and wholly inartistic
produce, encouraged mannerism, frowned on work from nature and
suppressed minor originality.    The practice agreed better with mural
than with easel work.    Such decoration is not to be seen close, it is
shown usually in a bad light where the general design rather than the
quality of the execution is of supreme concern.    Such work enjoys the
immunities and displays the defects of a public speech compared with a
carefully-written and carefully-read poem or narrative.    Justify his
practice how we may, yet the difficulties of studying Rubens are no whit
the less great, especially as one has to count with his slow and gradual
change of style.

The enormous number of his works or reputed works, and the many
and wide-apart places where they are kept, add much to the trouble of
studying Rubens.    To separate the good from the bad, the work of
pupils from that of the master, to discover the real Rubens, to elucidate
his various manners, to conceive a just estimate of his genius, becomes
an almost impossible task when his pictures are so numerous and so
widely separated.    Mr. Max Rooses has done more than any one to
complete the study of Rubens from the point of view of research.
Eugène Delacroix and Fromentin have given the most painter-like
criticisms of the artist's work.    Rooses, after fifteen years of travel and
study, has compiled, in the five volumes of his *L'Œuvre de Rubens*,
his researches into the history of more than a thousand works.    Moreover, he has arranged, in the ground-floor of the new gallery at Antwerp,
a collection of photographs and engravings embracing the whole achieve-
ment of Rubens.    Yet in this man's opinion the final work on the
subject has not yet appeared, although he admits that the future historian

of Rubens will find facilities and advantages that none of his predecessors enjoyed. No small capacity or common qualifications are demanded of the man who would worthily follow Rooses, Fromentin, Henri Hymans, Piot, Charles Ruelens, and the men who have gone before them. He must be a painter with Fromentin's insight, feeling, and literary gift ; like Rooses, he must be a student and a linguist ; before all, he must be a man of means, independent of paying work, a man who can live for long periods in every large city of Europe, a man of energy who can revisit them in a year and gather up all the pictures in a final swoop of comparison. Rooses complains of the long intervals that elapsed between the pictures he saw when he was new to the task, and those he saw towards the end of his work. He confesses that without the money voted him by Antwerp for travelling expenses he could not have accomplished what he has done.

England abounds in pictures by Rubens. The National Gallery has more than twenty ; the Dulwich and Cambridge Museums and many private collections possess examples, as those of the Queen, the Duke of Westminster, the Duke of Norfolk, Lord Ashburton, the late Sir Richard Wallace, the Duke of Devonshire, Earl Spencer, Earl of Warwick, Duke of Rutland, Duke of Marlborough, Mr. Charles Butler, Sir T. Baring, Sir Philip Miles, the Duke of Hamilton, the Duke of Bedford, Lord Northbrook, Lord Pembroke, Lord Darnley, Lord Lonsdale, Lord Carlisle, Sir Watkins Wynn, the Holford Collection, and I believe some others. The Prado (Madrid) and the Hermitage (St. Petersburg) each contains about eighty pictures, the Louvre more than sixty, the Pinakothek (Munich) ninety, Dresden forty-eight, Berlin twenty-five, Brussels thirty-seven, the galleries of Vienna seventy or eighty, the Hague eleven, and even Stockholm fifteen ; add to these more than twenty or thirty in Italy and you have not then told the tale. New York and Chicago have pictures, while the collections of drawings at Vienna, Paris, London and elsewhere run up to a great number. It will be seen that our National Gallery cannot give an adequate view of Rubens. What we have is, on the whole, very good ; but the pictures are small and mostly of one sort. Without going far, however, one can increase one's knowledge, and I should say go hand-in hand with Fromentin to Flanders. His *Maîtres d'Autrefois* will fill you with some enthusiasm for the art of Rubens. Until one cares for his pictures and knows Rubens well by the eye, the scholarship of the subject seems a meaningless repetition of subtilties encased purposely in a horny shell. To the unsophisticated lover of beautiful things, to the tired man of business on a holiday, these interminable descriptions of pictures, confirmations of dates, disjointed notes and cross references to the obscure points of history, appear as steep reading as a financial journal. With very little practical knowledge or interest, perhaps with close study of one picture by Rubens, any man can read and enjoy the eloquent Fromentin. Antwerp is now the best place to begin on. There you may see the chief pictures that mark the beginnings and the ends of Rubens's consecutive manners— *The Elevation of the Cross, The Descent from the Cross, The Adoration of the Magi, The Assumption of the Virgin,* and *The Virgin and Saints* of the Rubens Chapel in St. Jacques' Church.

After the picture gallery in the Museum you can consult the collection of photographs and engravings with the aid of Max Rooses' small catalogue. If the inoculation takes, you will become an enthusiast, and you will visit, as far as you can, Brussels, Malines, Paris, Munich, Madrid, etc. You may even read the Rubens literature. Early and contemporary works that speak of Rubens are not lacking. There are the memoirs of the painter by his nephew Philippe Rubens, and by his friend Giovanni Baglione. There are also the more general works of Joachim Sandrart, de Piles, Van Mander, and others of the seventeenth century. In the eighteenth we have F. Mols, J. F. Michel, and two or three more. Near 1840 many books were published about Rubens, notably that by Waagen, and also several collections of his letters. Amongst later and more or less careful and trustworthy books we may mention Emile Gachet's *Unpublished Letters of Rubens,* Bruxelles, 1840 ; W. H. Carpenter's Extracts from Original Documents in the State Paper Office, London, 1844 ; W. Noel Sainsbury's *Unpublished Original Papers relating to Rubens,* London, 1849 ; Armand Baschet's articles in the *Gazette des Beaux Arts,* Paris, 1866-68 ; Villaamil's *Rubens diplomatico español,* Madrid, 1874 ; Gachard's *Histoire politique de Rubens,* Brussels, 1877 ; J. A. X. Michiel's *Rubens et l'École d'Anvers,* 4th edition, 1877 ; Charles Ruelens's *Correspondance de Rubens, etc.,* Anvers, 1887 ; Max Rooses' *L'Œuvre de Rubens,* Anvers, 1886-92 ; Henri

Hymans's *Histoire de la gravure dans l'École de Rubens*, Bruxelles, 1879; *Un Rubens à retrouver*, 1892; *Un voyage ignoré de Rubens*, 1893; and other papers and pamphlets on Northern Art. It seems scarcely necessary to say that this monograph contains no new facts or discoveries; indeed, nothing that may not be found with trouble in the books just mentioned.

# CHAPTER I

*Childhood and youth of Rubens—His early studies—His masters--His Italian sojourn—His work, study, and travel in Italy and Spain.*

THE ancestors of Peter Paul Rubens were burgesses of Antwerp, tanners by their way of life. Michel, a fantastic biographer of Rubens in the last century, gives the family a more aristocratic origin ; but the fact is that John Rubens (1530-87), the father of the great painter, was the first of them to follow any other than an industrial career. In those days custom sent the learned and the artistic who desired consideration in their profession to Rome, the centre of all things ; and the elder Rubens, a scholar and man of letters, did his seven years in Italy, where he took a degree of Doctor of Laws. Upon his return in 1561 he married Marie Pypelinckx (1538-1608), a woman of strong and decided character, by whom he had several children, and first among them John, who was born in 1562, and died in 1600.

Not much is known with certainty of the life of the family ; but certainly it was not tranquil in such disturbed times. Michiels says that the father of Rubens reached prosperity and became a man of note and an alderman (*échevin*) in his native town ; he was a Protestant, however, and in 1568 the religious and political troubles of the Spanish rule drove him with his family to Cologne. John Rubens, like Peter Paul, appears to have possessed the knack of getting on with princes, and of making himself agreeable to great ladies. Hence much sorrow, for he was less lucky, as well as less prudent, than his greater son. In exile he soon became the intimate counsellor of William the Silent, Prince of Orange, and his wife Anne, daughter of the Elector of Saxony. Unhappily the father of the irresistible artist was himself prepossessing, while the princess was by nature treacherous and inflammable.

The elder Rubens could not resist the flattery of a royal conquest, and under the cover of business matters the doctor and the princess conducted a clandestine love affair. All went well for a while, till the absence of the prince, too much prolonged by heroic warfare, made the condition of Anne a manifest scandal in the eyes of her parents and her husband's friends. The doctor was torn from his unsuspecting wife and flung into prison, and but for her devoted efforts he might have lost his life instead of his liberty. To help his case Dr. Rubens himself could think of nothing better than to remind the outraged prince of all the great men in history that had suffered a like wrong with equanimity, and to console him with the assurance that the indignity might easily have been greater since some authorities rank a doctor of laws only just below a baron. From this story one gathers that the doctor, by his natural gifts and bearing, bred confidence in men and princes, affection in his wife, and passion in a great lady ; while by his overlay of learning he exposed himself to contempt as a fool and an insufferable prig. His education had not developed his nature, but had buried it in a foreign and artificial culture. When the prince divorced Anne and married again, John Rubens was released, though under various restrictions as to his place of residence. It is certain that he died in Cologne on the 1st of March 1587.

We should say that Ruelens never even alludes to this pretty story, and, indeed, states expressly that very little reliable material exists for an account of the infancy of Rubens and the wanderings of his father's family. Between the rival claims of Antwerp, Siegen, and Cologne to be the birthplace of P. P. Rubens, Ruelens inclines to favour that of Antwerp. He thinks that when Peter Paul was a year old the Rubenses migrated from Antwerp to Cologne, and stayed there until the death of the father in 1587. He seems not even sure of the father's profession ; for in the records of Cologne during these years two painters, father and son, by name Jean Robins, are mentioned as paying taxes to the town. In 1586 the eldest brother of Peter Paul went to Italy in the usual way and disappeared for ever, at least from historical records. After the death of their father, Marie Pypelinckx brought back to Antwerp her surviving children—Philippe, born in 1574; Peter Paul, born in 1577; and their sister Blandina (1564-1606), who married Siméon du Parcq in 1590. The boys were sent to a good school, where they were well grounded in the classics and brought up among the sons of well-to-do citizens. Balthazar Moretus, one of these early companions of the Rubens boys, was the grandson of the famous printer of Antwerp, Christopher Plantin. Moretus became a man of letters, and later on, with Philippe Rubens and John Wouverius, he joined the band of learned men who gathered round the celebrated Professor Justus Lipsius at Louvain. B. Moretus afterwards carried on the family printing business in the beautiful old house still preserved in Antwerp under the name of the Musée Plantin. It is full of relics of Rubens, his work, his friendships ; and if you wish to call up a vision of the Antwerp of his day you must visit the house of his friends, a house that still bears traces of their occupation in every room, and on its walls their portraits by the hand of Peter Paul himself.

When he left school, Rubens had a short experience of etiquette as page of honour to the Princess Margaret de Ligne-Aremberg. Probably his mother referred to this service when she says in a letter written at the time of her daughter's marriage that her sons were already earning their living. Useful as the sight of Court life must have been to one destined to live among princes, it cannot have been more than a peep, since in the year 1591 Rubens began his professional studies as a painter.

Tobias Verhaeght (1561-1631), the husband of Rubens's cousin, Suzanne van Mockenborch, had just returned from Italy, and naturally enough it was to him that the young painter turned for professional teaching in his art. Verhaeght, a landscape man, had won some success in Rome with his *Tower of Babel*, a picture which was furnished with figures by his countryman Sebastien Franck. Collaboration in picture-making, whether between master and pupil, or between two specialists, obtained the sanction of artists and patrons long before the time of Rubens, though he himself possibly carried it to greater lengths than any of his predecessors. The practice agreed fairly well with the nature of the ecclesiastical and palatial art of the times. The successful artist became a kind of *entrepreneur*, who undertook the conduct of all sorts of decoration, and provided men to carry out his designs. Art was not so generally understood then as now to mean the expression of a poetic person's individual feelings. For this reason the best and most personal work of Rembrandt, a more modern man than Rubens, met during his lifetime with something like coldness and neglect. Rubens remained not longer than six months under the care of his first master ; probably he felt himself drawn to figure work both by interest and by inclination, but it is worth while remembering the nature of the first studies of a man who was destined to produce the finest and most original landscape that had been hitherto executed.

From Verhaeght Rubens passed to Adam van Noort, a man twenty years his elder, who nevertheless just outlived his ennobled and illustrious pupil. Van Noort did not belong to the polished, learned, perhaps somewhat affected society in which the young Rubenses were brought up, doubtless owing to their father's reputation and relations amongst men of letters. On the contrary, he was a rude Fleming, whose moroseness led him to drink, whose drunkenness made him violent or cantankerous. Rubens could support the manners of such a boor with less convenience than the coarser-fibred Jordaens, a later pupil, who became the son-in-law of Van Noort. This dainty bud that was to unfold into the full-blown Rubens, the courtly favourite of kings, the knightly ambassador and the discreet counsellor of secret conferences, must have been nipped and chilled in the rude boisterous atmosphere of a studio of young Flemings, presided over by a tipsy sot who passed rapidly from rough gin-bred joviality to savage fits of gloomy fury. However, Rubens was young, and, though externally refined, stout enough in texture to put up with four or five years of this unpleasant discipline.

In 1596 the young painter became pupil of a man of his own kidney, one well fitted to forward his ambitions and to inspire him with a love of Italy and a respect for tradition. Otho van Veen (1558-1629), called Vaenius after the Latin fashion, which made Gevaerts Gevartius and Rubens Rubenius, was a scholar and a gentleman as well as a disciplined figure painter. According to the legend of his family, Van Veen had royal blood in his veins. His ancestress, Isabeau van Veen, was mistress of John III., Duke of Brabant. This third master of Rubens was a learned and accomplished person, filled with classic receipts and precepts, a student cultivated by foreign travel in Italy and Germany, a pupil of the Zuchero who painted our Queen Elizabeth, and a friend of Justus Lipsius and other scholars who formed the upper crust of Flemish literary society. After life in the studio of Van Noort, the tutelage of Vaenius must have expanded the talent of Rubens as a blossom opens in the first genial warmth of spring. No doubt Vaenius was a dull painter, a somewhat lifeless copyist of his Italian masters, even a bit of a pedant perhaps ; but then his pupil had not yet seen Italy, and was accustomed to pedantry from his childhood. Method he would learn from Vaenius, the topography of the Italian pictures and statues, the speculations and the gossip of Italian artists, the bearing and habits of a man of the world to which he was inclined by nature ; and lastly, a further initiation into that classic literature and mythology which he had begun at school.

Rubens stayed four years with Vaenius, and towards the middle of this period, just as he came of age, he was received as a *franc-maître* of the gild of St. Luke. This Society was described in its charter as a reunion of *honnétes bourgeois*, and it included, in addition to those men we now call artists, all kinds of craftsmen, such as printers, potters, gold-beaters, type-founders, and makers of carpets, curtains, playing-cards, etc. The gild imposed strict rules on its members, which bore severely on artists, and from this tyranny they were only emancipated by appointment as painter to the sovereign. Rubens was now a full-grown man, still working with Vaenius, though enrolled amongst the artists of his native town and about to practise on his own account. In appearance he was large and fair, with that mixture of swagger and sensitive refinement that one often remarks in the heads of artists. He had bold features, with the gentle bovine eye that he liked to bestow on the personages of his pictures. His looks altogether were such as might recommend him anywhere, not least amongst the great ; since the original nobility of Northern Europe came for the most part from big-made, light-haired, and sanguine races. Nor were his manners likely to shake the confidence inspired by his looks. Probably even in youth he was not one to wear his heart on his sleeve, to babble in low company, or to miss the right measures of reserve and openness, dignity, and respect in his attitude towards those of superior rank or reputation. Moreover, he was accomplished ; he spoke and wrote Latin, Greek, French, and Italian, besides Flemish and Spanish, although it must be said that whatever tongue he used, in his letters at least, he was seldom communicative, gushing, garrulous or even entertaining. His letters lack personal interest, warm feeling, picturesque expression of any kind. Indeed, he shows as little of himself in them as he possibly can, and writes for duty or for business purposes. Most of

TWO STUDIES OF A BOAR'S HEAD. *British Museum.*

his very intimate correspondence, however, has perished; for instance, all that addressed to his mother, his wives, or his children. Judging by what is left, one could not call him anything but a lifeless writer; written words are evidently no natural outlet for his feelings.

We know but little of Rubens as a painter during this period (1596-1600). Max Rooses mentions three or four pictures that were probably painted before 1600, but, owing to doubtful evidence and possible repainting, he thinks them insufficient ground for opinion, and accepts Philippe Rubens's statement that Peter Paul's early work resembled that of his master Otto Vaenius. An *Annunciation* in the Imperial Museum at Vienna (2.24 metres × 2 metres) seems the best example of this early period. It is very coloured, very artificial, very Italian, and in mere composition not unlike a later picture in the Dublin Gallery. Rooses considers that the Vienna picture may be one that Rubens painted before 1600 for the Jesuits' literary society in Antwerp. He mentions also as possibly of this period *Pausias and Glycera*, belonging to the Duke of Westminster; *Christ and Nicodemus*, in the collection of Madame von Parys at Brussels; and a *Crowning of the Virgin* in the Hermitage, St. Petersburg.

Philip II. of Spain before he died in 1598 married his daughter Isabella Clara Eugenia to Albert, son of Maximilian II., Emperor of Germany, and gave the royal couple the sovereignty of Spanish Flanders. Liberty, tolerance, and prosperity were expected from their reign; and their entrance to Antwerp in 1599 was the cause of public rejoicing. Rubens must have lent a hand to the festal decorations which were entrusted to his master Vaenius, and must thus have gained some experience of a kind of work in which he was to excel afterwards. Without doubt he was presented as a young man of promise to his future patrons Albert and Isabella; indeed, some think that he may have met another patron, the Duke of Mantua, who visited Antwerp in 1599.

Twenty-three years old, son of a Roman Doctor of Laws, friend and brother of scholars, pupil of a learned and travelled painter, Rubens was ready to seize the first opportunity of making the classic journey to Italy. Who sent him is not known; but on the 9th of May 1600 he set out on his travels, and if he ventured on his own account he had not long to wait for a patron. When Vincenzo I. di Gonzaga, Duke of Mantua

(1562-1612), the son of Guglielmo di Gonzaga, and Eleanor, daughter of the Emperor Ferdinand I., met Rubens, he seems to have been taken as much by his manners and his Latin scholarship as by his skill in painting. Vincenzo was a clever man, fond of art and letters, indeed of anything that gave style and splendour to his pleasures, his entertainments, and his profuse way of life. His taste for show, whether in war or gallantry, often led him into financial trouble; but it is to his credit that he befriended Tasso, employed Pourbus the portrait painter, and was the first patron of Rubens.

Accounts differ as to the meeting of Rubens and the Duke. Some suppose that Rubens took Paris on his way to Italy and was presented to his patron in that city. Others—and this is the more probable view—hold that he went straight to Venice, where his copies of Titian and Veronese attracted the attention of a gentleman in the Duke's service. Others again will have it that the Archduke Albert furnished the painter with letters of recommendation to the Duke of Mantua. Ruelens has collected all the correspondence of Rubens and his friends which bears upon the Italian sojourn, but the first of their letters, from Balthazar Moretus to Philippe Rubens, bears the date of 3rd November 1600. Now on the 5th October the Duke of Mantua, with Rubens in his train, was present in Florence at the marriage of Henry IV. of France (by proxy) to Marie de Medicis. Thus the correspondence begins too late to throw any light on the first meeting of the painter and his patron. Since Rubens was afterwards employed to commemorate this royal marriage by his art, the learned have balanced the probabilities of his seeing or speaking to his future patron Marie de Medicis. Surely we may dismiss the idea that a young painter not noble would be allowed to chat freely with a newly married Queen of France. People long after his death cannot help assuming that a great man in his lifetime was always patent to his contemporaries. It is not so nowadays; and, although one may meet one or two young men capable of doing works of genius, even should one recognise their latent power, one dare not prophesy how they will turn out under conflicting influences. Existing letters written by Rubens and his friends prove that the Flemish artist, although he had secured a royal patron, was not yet considered a greater man than other young painters of his time.

Perhaps the habit of writing in Latin somewhat tamed the corre-

spondence of Rubens, his brother, and his contemporaries. They may not
have been capable of such a priggish letter as the one sent by old John
Rubens to William the Silent, but they wrote in a cloistered spirit remote
from actuality as a man might speak whose conversation should have

*Sketch for the Elevation of the Cross. Louvre.*
*From a Photograph by Braun, Clément, & Cie.*

been always conducted in a serious London club. For a big and vital
being Rubens wrote tame letters; formal and mannered pages that tell
little of the writer and his feelings. His brother Philippe's are literary
productions still more correct and laboured. When he wrote from
Flanders on the 21st May 1601 to a brother who was newly plunged
into the full and exciting life that the two must have often pictured in

their intimate talk, Philippe elaborates a school essay on virtue, friend-ship, absence, which might have been written for a Latin prize. It abounds with allusions to Cicero, Homer, and Plato, and it is adorned with appropriate quotations from Greek and Latin authors. Philippe shows none of the overflowing interest in his brother's new life and new experiences that one would get from a young and intelligent Scot of our day ; none of the inquiring subtlety and confiding enthusiasm that one always expects from youth and friendship. By the light of such corre-spondence one sees Rubens in the midst of a circle of superior young men who pat each other on the back (in Latin) and pride themselves on belonging to an exclusive intellectual society. The coarser, baser, more natural roots of life in Flanders do not sprout spontaneously in the pretentious efforts at refinement of this coterie of select young men. Rude Belgium should have manured this flower of culture, which, however, was grown in Rome and exported like an exotic plant. The same thing goes on in English commercial towns to-day. Their culture is not the blossom of their lives ; it is not grown, but manufactured ; not indigenous, but imported. Belgian refinement also spoke art with a somewhat provincial accent ; for in the sixteenth and seventeenth centuries Brussels and Antwerp recognised Spain as a master and Italy as a finishing tutor; although at an earlier period it may be said with truth that Bruges had led an independent existence. Perhaps, then, it was well for Rubens and other artists to travel and live in the freer air of a country whose culture was to some extent the expression of its life and the decoration of its habits of thought and feeling. Two clubs promoted culture at Antwerp. When the travelled men returned to the North, in order to keep alive the sacred traditions in barbarous parts, they formed themselves into a club called the *Romanistes*. To some extent we have seen in our century a like spirit animating young painters who have studied in France, the modern centre of artistic enterprise. The other club was founded by the Jesuits, who possessed rich churches, and most of the patronage of art and literature. It was for this society that Rubens painted his first *Annunciation*.

Philippe Rubens soon followed his brother to Italy. While Peter Paul was a page of honour, his brother had entered the office of Jean Richardot, a councillor at Brussels and a man of wealth and importance.

SKETCH FOR A BOAR HUNT. *British Museum.*

Philippe shepherded his son William Richardot throughout Italy, starting in 1601 and returning in 1604. It was through the influence of the Richardot family that Peter Paul got his first Roman commission to paint pictures for the Church of the Holy Cross of Jerusalem at Rome. On the 18th of July 1601 the Duke of Mantua, who was to pay for the pictures, sent Rubens (*un Flamand mon peintre*) with a letter of introduction to Cardinal Montalto. Rubens set to work upon a central piece, *St. Helen finding the True Cross*, flanked by a *Crown of Thorns*, and an *Elevation of the Cross*. The works, after much wandering, are now in the Chapel of the Hospital at Grasse, Alpes Maritimes.

Whilst he was in Rome Rubens made friends with several artists, amongst others with "Velvet" Brueghel, who was to be his collaborator in many pictures, and with Giovanni Baglione, a painter who became his earliest biographer. In the spring of the following year Rubens was recalled to Mantua, soon to depart for Venice and Padua, where a man of his taste for scientific research would be sure to seek an introduction to Galileo, who was only about thirteen years his senior. Rubens took a keen pleasure in the discoveries of science, and it is probable, as we shall find later, that his profession of religion and his attendance at mass were rather outward conformities expected from a respectable church painter and a subject of the King of Spain than the outward manifestations of orthodox conviction or deep-seated Catholic bigotry. His father had professed both religions in turn, and possibly his son, the humanist painter, took religion as a matter of course without conscious dissimulation, as one takes the necessary evils of calling and polite conversation.

In the summer of this same year, 1602, Rubens joined his brother's party at Verona. Here they met Wouverius, like Philippe a favourite pupil of Justus Lipsius, and Rubens took occasion to paint the interesting picture *Justus Lipsius and his Pupils*, now in the Pitti Palace, Florence. Lipsius faces you at the head of a table ; on his right sits Philippe, on his left Wouverius, while Rubens himself stands at a little distance drawing back a curtain.

Rubens was soon once more at the Court of Mantua working at his usual business, portrait-painting. Vincenzo I., like other great persons, sent his portrait to friends and allies, and was himself desirous of possessing likenesses of celebrated people or beautiful ladies. In a letter to his agent and ambassador Iberti, Vincenzo says of Rubens, "The above-mentioned P. P. R. succeeds perfectly with portraiture." This Iberti as the Duke's chief man had naturally very much to do with Rubens, and seems to have been one of those few whose favour the painter could not win by the prudence of his behaviour or the charm of his manner. On the other hand, he made a conquest of the Duke's secretary Annibale Chieppio, afterwards Minister and Count. It is to this Chieppio that Rubens addresses most of his letters, whether written to give an account of his proceedings or to ask for some favour, such as an extension of his leave of absence.

When the Duke sent Iberti in 1603 on a mission to Spain, Rubens was given charge of the presents of horses and pictures for the king Philip III., and his minister the Duke of Lerma. With the exception of a letter to the Duke himself, it is to Chieppio that Rubens writes the description of his voyage and the account of his expenses. On the 18th of March he mentions that he has run short of money in Florence; at Pisa he tells of an audience with the Grand Duke Ferdinand I., son of Cosmo de' Medici, and he explains that his heavy expenses are unavoidable: "the keep of the horses is sumptuous but necessary; it includes bottles of wine and other costly attentions." The verse that sends rain to Spain is justified by the rhyme; but on Rubens's journey twenty-five days of continued wet proved it to be also based on reason. The canvases in his care suffered grievously from the damp, and some of them required repainting. Rubens declined the job, as he tells Chieppio "having always followed the rule not to confound myself with another man, however great." The use he made later on of pupils and assistants shows that he had no objection to confound another man with himself: he disliked his work to pass as another's; he did not mind that another's should be called his. Rubens, however, painted *Heraclitus Crying* and *Democritus Laughing* to replace two of the damaged pictures which had been sent to the first minister, the Duke of Lerma. Whilst at Valladolid he did other work for the Duke of Lerma, a series, *Christ and the Twelve Apostles*, and also a portrait of the Duke on horseback. Besides the prime minister he painted many of the Spanish nobles, but on this first visit he was not considered worthy to work directly for the king; indeed he complains to Chieppio that Iberti had not yet presented him to His

*The Descent from the Cross.   Antwerp Cathedral.*
*From the Engraving by L. Vorsterman.*

Majesty. As to the Spanish painters of that date, he seems to have thought too poorly of them to wish to be associated with them in any work "connaissant l'incroyable insuffisance et la paresse de ces peintres dont la manière d'ailleurs—et ceci est important—diffère complètement de la mienne ; Dieu me garde de leur ressembler en quoi que ce soit." If he did not like the local painting he admired the imported Italian work, and spoke warmly of the Titians, Raphaels, and other pictures at the Escurial and the king's palace.

On his return to Italy Rubens appears to have passed a year or so (1604-6) quietly working for Vincenzo di Gonzaga at Mantua. To this period is assigned the *Trinity*, now in the Library of Mantua. The picture has been cut into two pieces, which are placed at the ends of the room. Each half measures 190 centimetres by 250 ; the upper contains the Trinity, and the lower four worshippers : on the left Vincenzo and his father, on the right his mother Eleanor, daughter of Ferdinand I., and his second wife Leonora de' Medici. Though damaged and repainted Rooses considers this picture, especially the lower half, one of the best specimens of Rubens's Italian work. The *Baptism of Christ* in the Antwerp Museum and the *Transfiguration* at Nancy also belong to this period.

The painter revisited Rome, probably by way of Venice ; at any rate he was in the capital by 29th July 1606, a date on which he writes to Chieppio. In December of the same year he asks for extended leave of absence to finish the work he has undertaken at S. Maria in Vallicella (Chiesa Nuova). He completed and set up his *Madonna*, an altar-piece on canvas, and in July 1607 he accompanied his ducal patron to Genoa, passing through Milan, where he copied Leonardo da Vinci's *Last Supper*.

At Genoa Rubens made several rich friends, for the most part merchants or bankers, such as the Pallavicini, who were afterwards of service to him. For the Jesuits, his constant patrons, he painted several works, and a *Circumcision*, which was paid for by the Marquis Nicolas Pallavicini. Rooses thinks that the *Last Judgment* in the Balbi Palace, Genoa, and the *Fall of the Wicked* at Aix-la-Chapelle in the Suermondt Collection, may both date from this visit to Genoa. In this case they would be the first attempts on a small scale at rendering the complicated figure subjects which Rubens afterwards treated on the huge canvases now at Munich. At any rate, they show his worst faults, from which indeed the larger versions are scarcely free ; bad taste, lack of unity, and a kind of tame imitation of Michael Angelo. The *Assumption of the Just*, Pinakothek, Munich, is another small version of a large canvas which may possibly belong to the Italian period. It looks like a rain of little nude figures, and as a pattern soon becomes extremely wearisome. In addition to these labours, Rubens, while in Genoa, occupied himself in the study of architecture, and made drawings of palaces, which were afterwards engraved at Antwerp.

In February 1608 we hear again of Rubens from Rome. He tells Chieppio that most people praise his altar-piece in the Chiesa Nuova, but that, in his opinion, the light from the church windows striking on the oil paint produces disadvantageous reflections. He suggests that the Duke of Mantua should buy the canvas from him, saying, as an inducement, that it contains a number of figures, but no emblems which would prevent them from passing for other Saints. The Duke was not seduced by this offer ; perhaps he was short of money, perhaps he was enlightened enough to doubt the value of quantity in figure-painting, or perhaps he held the advanced idea that figures should not require emblems to determine their character. Rubens kept the canvas, and when his mother died he placed it over her tomb. Meanwhile he began upon the new picture, a *Madonna surrounded by Angels*, which still remains above the altar of the Chiesa Nuova. He painted it upon slabs of slate, that the colour might lie smooth and sink in so as to make the reflections less destructive. He says, with more practical sense than enthusiasm, " I need not trouble myself to make it very good or highly finished, because no one can ever judge of it in this bad light." Rooses calls it a work of little importance, which scarcely shows the hand of Rubens. On the right of the high altar of this church the painter put a picture of *St. Gregory*, accompanied by two other Saints ; on the left a canvas with Saints, *Donatilla, Nerea*, and *Achillea*. That of *St. Gregory* was not finished when the painter heard of his mother's last illness. He at once set out for Antwerp, taking the unfinished canvas with him, but he arrived too late to see Marie Pypelinckx, who died on 19th October 1608. Rubens, who was always sensible to the family affections, took this loss very much to heart. He remained in strict seclusion for several months,

THE DEFEAT OF SENNACHERIB. *Albertina, Vienna.*

*From a photograph by Braun, Clément & Cie.*

and when he reappeared in the world he would have returned to his service with the Duke of Mantua. This, however, was not to be ; his journeyings to and fro were over for many years, and he was destined to pass a long time in the quiet pursuit of his art. The stadtholders, Albert and Isabella, perceived his growing reputation, and to attach the painter to their service they offered him, with a salary of five hundred florins, the appointment of court painter, which made him independent of the restrictions of the gild of St. Luke.

Rubens, however, had no wish to join the court at Brussels, so he was permitted to live and work in Antwerp. Probably he felt the need of quiet, the power to dispose of his own time, and the opportunity to digest the impressions and experiences of his late studies and travels. Moreover, he had friends in Antwerp, and especially his brother Philippe, for whose book on Rome he had made a few illustrations before he left Italy. These are supposed to be the earliest engraved work of Rubens. Philippe, who had just been made one of the secretaries of the town, was married to Maria de Moy, daughter of the chief secretary ; and it was probably at her house that Rubens saw and admired her niece Isabella Brant, daughter of John Brant, a lawyer. Rubens and Isabella were married in St. Michael's Church on the 13th of October 1609, and they went to live with John Brant until they had a house of their own. The following year the painter designed and built a kind of Italian palace in the street now called Rubens Street ; the building contained a magnificent staircase, a fine studio, and a gallery for the pictures, marbles, bronzes, etc., which the painter had collected in Italy.

# CHAPTER II

*His first marriage—His life in Antwerp—His first journey to Holland—Rubens and his pupils and collaborators—Pictures, portraits, and drawings of the second period.*

THIS is an important moment in Rubens's history. He has returned full of experience to settle in his native town ; he is just married and established in a house of his own ; he has won some reputation in Italy and Spain ; he has acquired knowledge of the world and of his art, and he is about to enter on his second manner of painting which emancipated Flemish art, founded the Antwerp school, and captivated the world. Rubens must have had his hands full, settling his life, arranging his purchases, overhauling his sketches, to say nothing of executing the numerous commissions which began to shower upon the successful painter. With his excellent sense he ordered his life upon a prudent system. In the morning he rose very early, and while he painted some one read aloud Livy, Plutarch, Cicero, Virgil or other poets. Then he would stroll in his gallery to stimulate his taste by the sight of the works of art he had brought from Italy. On other occasions he would study science, in which he always retained an active interest. Although he lived splendidly, he ate and drank moderately ; and the gout from which he suffered in later life was certainly undeserved. He painted in the afternoon till towards evening, when he mounted a horse and rode out of the town. His inclination took him often along the embankment of the Scheldt below Antwerp. Here one is a little raised above the country and the river; the first seems sad and quiet, the other alive with shipping and the Dutch barges that Cuyp and Van de Velde have often painted. Antwerp, gray and old, thrown into a close perspective, is entirely dominated by its weather-worn Cathedral tower. When I

*Rubens and his first Wife, Isabella Brant. Pinakothek, Munich.*
*From a Photograph by F. Hanfstaengl.*

lived in Antwerp I have often taken this walk in company with students of the Academy, enthusiastic admirers of Rubens. Legends of his life and work, often more picturesque than true, enlivened the endless discussion of art. Then, in 1873, the Quais were not disfigured by a line of iron sheds, and curious old houses still looked out upon the river.

During this more tranquil period, which covers at least the first ten or twelve years of Rubens's life after his return to Antwerp, the artist of course saw many friends of his own profession, such as Brueghel, Van Balen, Jordaens, and without doubt his old masters Van Noort and Vaenius. But through his brother and Balthazar Moretus he was also acquainted with men of letters and learning as well as those of eminence in the city—men such as Nicolas Rockox, burgomaster ; Paul Gevaerts (1593-1666), philosopher and secretary of the town ; F. Sweert, a historian and antiquary, and many other persons of note. The extent of his reading and the genuineness of his interest in archæology may be seen from his letters—for instance, from that written to Sweert in Latin about Isis and her symbols, or that later one of 10th August 1630 to Peiresc on the use and origin of various kinds of antique tripods. These letters in Sainsbury's *Original Papers relating to Rubens* are among the best written and the most interesting pages of the Rubens correspondence. The great painter was anything but excitable or frivolous, and his mind worked best upon a serious subject. Rubens painted or retouched portraits of many of these noted men, some of them, such as Justus Lipsius, at the request of Balthazar Moretus. Unhappily Philippe Rubens was soon lost to this studious society ; he died in 1611, leaving behind him a son who followed his father's profession of letters, and was the author of a Latin life of Peter Paul Rubens, a book of the greatest importance to the historical study of the painter.

So far, Rubens appears a somewhat solemn, studious, and courtly figure, better suited to the demure reserve of the diplomatic service than to the frank gaiety and the tavern manners which are generally ascribed to artists, and more particularly to the Dutch and Flemish painters. One wonders how he ever got through the ordeal of his student days ; but it must be remembered that Rubens was a politic person, able to control himself and to appear in many societies ; that we only hear of him through letters to literary men, politicians or patrons, or through the medium of writers who have every wish to show him only on one side of his character. It is said that he could not put up with the brutality of Van Noort, that he fled from the licentiousness of Margaret de Ligne's court. He stood the first inconvenience for four years, and when subjected to the second trial he was but a child of ten or twelve. Rubens undoubtedly presented a dignified and respectable front to the world; certainly he liked frugal living and the society of the learned, yet he could very well support the company of Adrian Brauwer, a notorious drunkard, to whom he was uniformly kind and serviceable. In fact, he was not such a bad comrade after all, and we have at least one episode to recount which shows him mingling in the gay, simple life of artists instead of sitting with compressed lips over state secrets at the council board, or meeting ministers and noblemen with respectful reserve or discreet affability.

Sandrart, a contemporary and a friend of the painter, had implied that the journey of 1627 was Rubens's first visit to Holland; Gachard discovered, in a letter of 30th September 1623, evidence that Rubens was in Holland at that date upon his first political mission. In 1893, however, Henri Hymans, a careful investigator of the history of Flemish art, published a pamphlet called *Un voyage ignoré de Rubens.* From a footnote to a poem by Balthasar Gerbier (1592-1667), political agent of the court of England, Hymans extracts the following passage:—" Rubens, Brueghel, Van Balen, and some other artists who were in Holland and had just left Haarlem, were surprised in a village on the road by Goltzius and a group of his friends disguised as peasants. This was done that they might do honour to the noble men of genius, and exchange with them, glass in hand, and with a rustic sort of frankness, a last assurance of friendship and faithful remembrance."

Now in October 1616 Sir Dudley Carleton, just landed as English Ambassador to the Hague, writes about the illness and the approaching death of the celebrated engraver Goltzius, who in fact died a month or two later on 1st January 1617. It is evident that the sick man could not have engaged in this artistic comedy, which reminds one of the effervescent manners of Marlotte in the time of Murger. Therefore, as Hymans says, we cannot put the date of the adventure later than 1615. It

TWO GIRLS. *Albertina, Vienna.*
From a photograph by Braun, Clément & Cie.

is the one sportive interlude in a steadily developing play of triumphant ambition.

As early as May 1611 Rubens writes to the engraver, J. de Bie, that he has been obliged to refuse more than a hundred would-be pupils. His great reputation, however, had not been won without arousing jealousies and enmities amongst the older painters. It was only by degrees that he became the quite undisputed head of the school ; only by the exercise of tact that he overcame envious opposition ; only by his wonderful influence over men of all ranks that he induced even fully established painters of his own age to work in his studio and to adopt his methods of painting. With some trouble at first, he persuaded both patrons and practitioners of art that subservience to his ideas of composition and execution was for the benefit of both parties. A story is told of the anger of the Dean of Malines Cathedral who had ordered a *Last Supper*, when, instead of Rubens, a young man, Justus von Egmont, came down and began the work. The Dean or Canon, with some difficulty, permitted the pupil to continue, but his fears were allayed when the great man appeared with his fine calm presence and the urbane manner that was a bulwark against offence or misappreciation. As Rubens corrected the work, enlivened the colour or the action of the figures and swept the whole composition with his unerring brushwork towards a beautiful unity of effect, the churchman acknowledged the wisdom of the master, and admitted that the money of the chapter had been safely invested.

To put it plainly, Rubens established a picture factory at Antwerp. He was thus enabled to paint portraits, landscapes, hunting scenes, and pictures of *genre*, as well as to undertake several series of gigantic decorations, as important as those of Raphael or Michael Angelo. The master made small, lively sketches of the work to be done, the pupils laid them in, each doing what suited his talent, while Rubens reserved to himself the duty of bringing the picture together ; in some cases by using the work beneath as a ground for almost complete repainting, in most cases by merely correcting here and there, or enhancing the effect with a few brilliant and dexterous touches. Might is right, but this was not Rubens's only justification, nor was the lust of money his sole reason for becoming an *entrepreneur* of these large jobs of decoration. The adornment of

c

ill-lit palaces and churches with scenes from the Bible or the lives of Saints, with royal marriages, and with the apotheoses of kings, demanded regulation figures, emblems, a method made to order, and a conventional line of treatment. The artist thus hampered might well adopt a reasoned and formal system of work which could be helped out by such pupils as he had trained to act as intelligent machines. By his manners, and the prestige of his reputation, Rubens increased the demand for art, and thus kept employed quiet, second-rate men who might otherwise have lacked work. His wholesale house for the ornamentation of palaces may have been admirably organised, may have been designed in an excellent and business-like fashion to satisfy the needs of his princely patrons, but it was not fitted to refine the genius of Rubens the painter, nor to make him an artistic rival of Velazquez and Rembrandt. When one remembers costly failures of riches and bad taste, such as the Ducal Palace and the Scuola di San Rocco, upon which nevertheless the best of men were employed, one feels that one would hang one's ideal palace with easel pictures in the common and unæsthetic fashion of our own day. But Rubens farmed out even his commissions for easel pictures, cabinet pictures, landscapes and portraits, with apparent satisfaction, a satisfaction that is not shared by those who have to look over his whole output. This calm man of business spread pictures over Europe in which his fine ideas were rendered in a second-rate manner, mechanically or tamely, and without conviction. Still it must be allowed that some half-hundred *chefs d'œuvre* of painting, as well as many drawings from nature, can be collected among his works to show the wonderful quality of his natural gifts. He had not the eye of Velazquez, the poetic perception of Rembrandt, but he had an artist's temperament that expressed itself in the language of paint with a florid and noble eloquence. His undoubted originality was less a new and individual way of seeing and composing the matter of nature than an original feeling for the use of paint, which under his hand at the moment expressed itself in a thousand felicities of handling and colouring. Was this man capable, like Raphael, of bearing translation at the hands of even the best-trained pupils? In their comparatively unimpassioned rendering the exuberance of his forms shocks and chills us instead of warming us to the due pitch of Rubensian vitality.

Sandrart, a friend and fellow-traveller of Rubens, has left a great deal

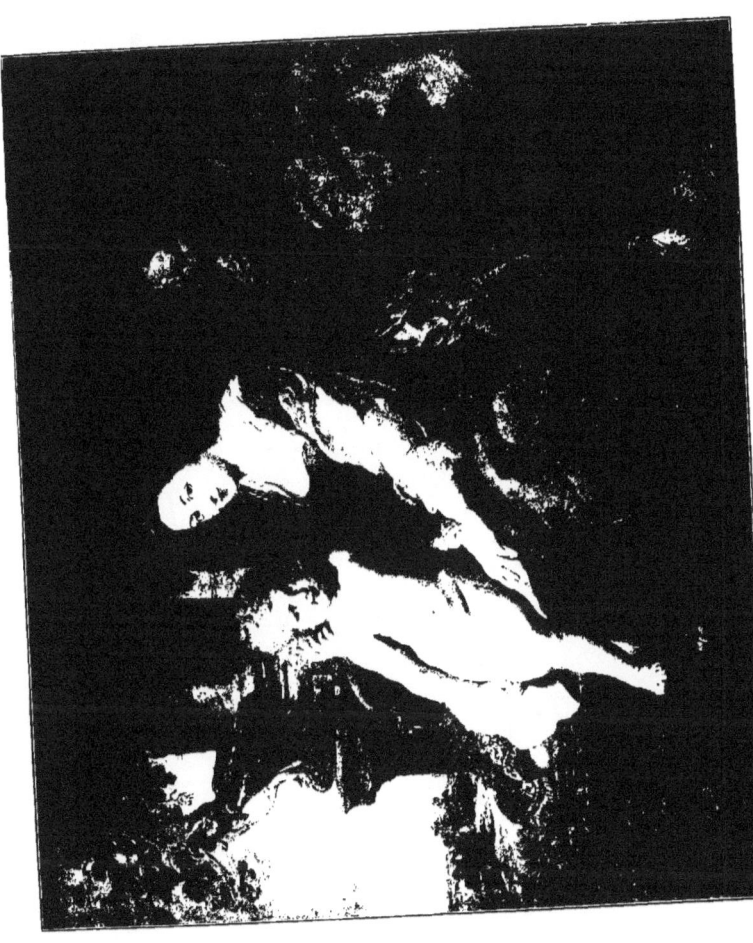

*La Vierge au Perroquet. Antwerp Museum. From a Photograph by Braun, Clément, & Cie.*

of information upon Claude, Rubens, and other seventeenth-century artists. He says that Rubens trained his pupils to do all the animals, birds, fish, trees, streams, grounds, waters and forests required in his pictures. Here are some of the special collaborators and pupils of Rubens—Brueghel (1568-1625), F. Snyders (1579-1657), Paul de Vos (157 -1678), A. Sallaert (1570-1632), J. Jordaens (1593-1678), Deodato

*Four Studies of a Negro's Head. Brussels Museum.*
*From a Photograph by G. Hermans.*

del Monte (1581-1644), Z. Seghers (1591-1651), Cornelius de Vos (1585-1651), Cornelius Schut (1597-1655), Abraham van Diepenbeck (1596-1675), Lucas van Uden (1695-1772), J. van den Hoecke (1611-51), A. van Dyck (1599-1641), Justus van Egmont (1602-74), Theodore van Thulden (1606-76), Erasmus Quellin (1607-78), D. Teniers (1610-90), Jan Fyt (1609-61), Jan Wildens (1586-1658). These men and many more all worked with or under Rubens, while Gasper de Crayer (1584-1669), T. Boeyermans (1620-78), J. Cossiers

(1600-71), Van Lint (1609-90), P. Thys (1624-79), are a few of
those who, if not all actual pupils, at any rate all learned their art from
the master's pictures.   Rubens himself had very little to learn except
rudiments from the Flemings who preceded him ; they were either
without science or without originality.

Of all the Rubens school Van Dyck is the best known and the most
interesting figure.   It is supposed that Van Dyck, after two years with
Henry van Balen, at the age of thirteen, in 1612, entered Rubens's
studio.   Jules Guiffrey, in his *Sir Anthony Van Dyck*, brings proof from
letters that this favourite pupil saw England before his master.   The
Earl of Arundel, whom Rubens called "the evangelist of the world of
art," was of course at the bottom of this visit.   Working through Sir
Dudley Carleton, ambassador at the Hague, he induced Van Dyck to
come to England about November 1620.   The painter made but a
short stay, and, soon after his return to Flanders, Van Dyck, in October
1621, left Rubens for Italy.   During this eight or nine years, however,
Van Dyck had done some important work for his master.   In 1618
Rubens made a series of designs for tapestries on the subject of the
devotion of Decius Mus, the Roman consul.   In a letter of 12th May
1618 Rubens gives Sir Dudley Carleton advice about buying tapestries,
and he mentions incidentally that he has just executed a set of superb
cartoons for tapestry at the order of certain Genoese noblemen.   These
designs, now for the most part in the Liechtenstein Gallery, Vienna, are
really noble pictures, which were laid in by Van Dyck from Rubens's
sketches and retouched by the master.   In 1620 a much larger contract
was offered Rubens by Father Tirinus, Superior of the Jesuits, for the
decoration of their church at Antwerp.   It was expressly stipulated that
Van Dyck should be one of the pupils employed, and that he should be
given the sole execution of "one of the pictures for the four small
altars of the church."   The whole series consisted of thirty-nine large
pictures, which, with the exception of four, perished in 1718, when the
church was burnt to the ground.   One of these four is lost ; three
remain in the Museum at Vienna, viz. an *Assumption of the Virgin*,
the *Miracles of St. Ignatius*, and the *Miracles of St. Francis Xavier*.
The compositions of the burnt pictures can be seen in thirty-six engravings, made by Jacob Punt from 1747 to 1763 after drawings in chalk,

STUDY FOR ST. CATHERINE.  *Albertina, Vienna.*

*From a photograph by Braun, Clément & Cie.*

now almost all destroyed, which Jacob de Wit took from the pictures themselves before the burning of the church.   Van Dyck's collaboration

*St. Martin dividing his Cloak with a Beggar.   Windsor Castle.*
*From a Photograph by F. Hanfstaengl.*

with his master and his imitation of his style make it difficult to separate their works.   For instance, Guiffrey and Rooses think that the *Brazen Serpent* at Madrid, a different arrangement from that in London, must be a work of imitation by Van Dyck.   As examples of a Rubens and its imitation by Van Dyck, Guiffrey points to the two *St. Jeromes* at Dresden. *St. Martin* (Windsor), supposed to be a Rubens, or at least a Rubens-Van Dyck collaboration, was copied by Van Dyck in his altar-piece—still in the church of Saventhem.  If you put the reproduction of the Windsor *St. Martin* in this monograph beside Boulard's etching of the Saventhem canvas in Guiffrey's book, you will wonder at the slightness of the changes, and perhaps think with Mr. Claude Phillips that Van Dyck painted both pictures.  Van Dyck probably helped his master in *Ambrose and Theodosius* (Vienna), and he certainly executed the reduced copy now in the National Gallery.

Van Dyck helped Rubens in smaller pictures, and also in his work for engravers.  It was the habit of Rubens to paint, or cause to be painted, small oil or water-colour sketches in monochrome for the use of the school of engravers whom he had trained to reproduce his works. Thus he himself kept control of that difficult part of engraving, the translation of colour values into black and white values.  Of these numerous engravers Vorsterman, according to Philippe Rubens the younger, was the chief up to 1623, when at his death Pontius and Bolswert took his place.  It is because these engravers worked not from the picture, but from a design specially made for their benefit, that the reproduction of a Rubens picture often differs greatly from the original work.  See for instance the *Jardin d'Amour* (Madrid) or the *Assumption of the Virgin* (Brussels) and their seventeenth-century engravings.

That Rubens employed collaborators and set his pupils to work from his designs is not altogether a matter of guesswork.  Besides the testimony of contemporary painters, such as Sandrart, we have letters to that effect from the master's own hand.  One or two, as they contain allusions to well-known pictures, may be quoted.  In April 1618 Rubens was negotiating with Sir Dudley Carleton an exchange of his pictures for the ambassador's antique marbles.  In a letter of the 18th the painter offers the following pictures : "A *Prometheus Enchained on Mount Caucasus*, with an eagle which devours his liver ; an original work of my own hand, the eagle done by Snyders, 500 florins.  *Daniel* in the midst of many lions, done from nature ; original work entirely by my hand, 600 florins.  *Leopards* painted from nature, with Satyrs and Nymphs ; original picture by my hand, except a fine landscape

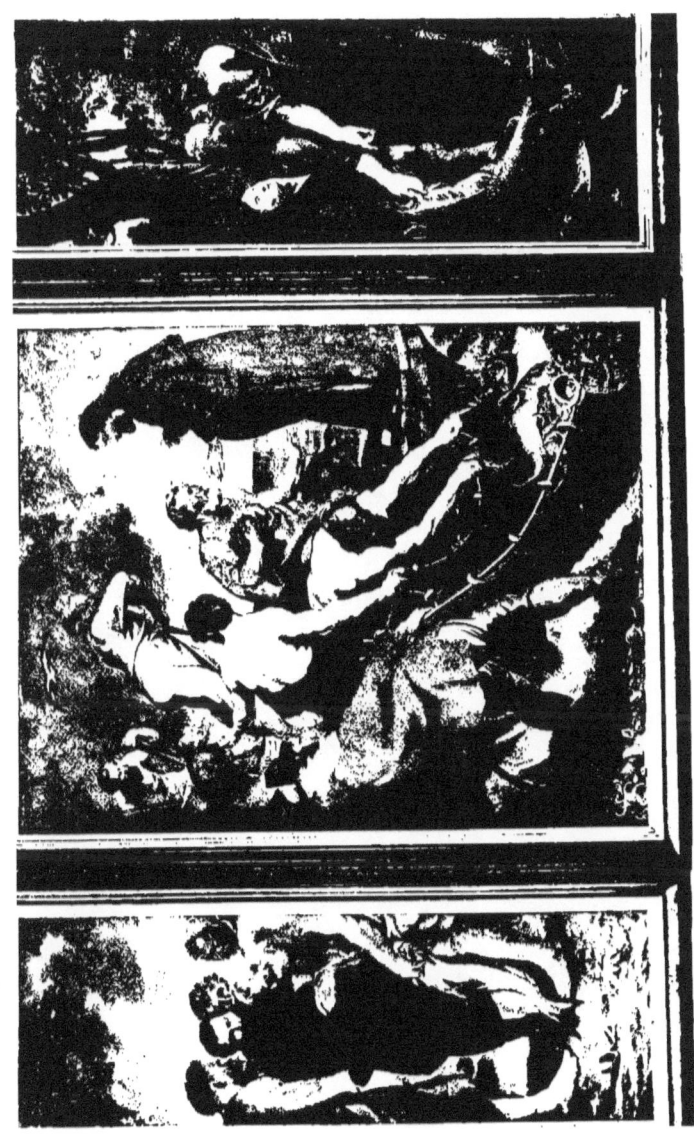

*The Miraculous Draught of Fishes. Church of Notre Dame, Malines. From a Photograph by G. Hermans.*

done by an artist clever at these kind of works, 600 florins.  *Leda, the Swan, and a Cupid;* original work by my own hand, 500 florins.  *Christ on the Cross,* life-size, considered perhaps the best thing I have ever done, 500 florins.  A *Last Judgment,* begun by one of my pupils after an original which I made of much larger size for the Prince of Neubourg, who paid me for it 3500 florins in ready money.  As the present piece is not quite finished, I will retouch it altogether by myself, so that it

*The Miraculous Draught of Fishes.  Copy by Van Dyck, with alteration.  National Gallery.
From a Photograph by Morelli.*

can pass for an original, 1200 florins.  *St. Peter* taking the coin out of the fish to pay the tribute, whilst other fishermen stand round him ; painted from nature, an original work of my own hand, 500 florins. *A Hunting-piece with Horsemen and Lions,* begun by one of my pupils after a picture which I did for the Duke of Bavaria ; it has, however, been entirely retouched by me, 600 florins.  *The Twelve Apostles with a Christ,* executed by my pupils after originals by me, belonging to the Duke of Lerma ; but I have retouched all these copies entirely with my own work.  Each fifty florins.  *A Piece representing Achilles disguised*

*as a Woman*, painted by my best pupil and entirely retouched by me ;
a very agreeable picture, and full of graceful young girls, 600 florins.
*St. Sebastian*, a nude, my own work, 300 florins. *Susanna and the Elders*,
the work of one of my pupils, but entirely retouched by my hand, 300
florins." Comment is unnecessary, especially as Rubens is still more
explicit in a letter of 11th October 1619 to the Duke of Bavaria, mentioned
in the foregoing list : "As to the *St. Michael*, the subject is very fine,
but very difficult, so I doubt that I shall find easily amongst my pupils
one capable of carrying it out satisfactorily even after my own drawing.
In any case it will be necessary for me to touch it up carefully with my
own hand."

Perhaps the most important allusion in these letters is that which
proves the *Last Judgment* in the Pinakothek, Munich, to have been
painted before 28th April 1618. This is one of Rubens's big canvases,
605 × 474 c.m. ; it is the largest of several of the same kind painted
probably in emulation of the *Paradise* of Tintoretto and the *Last
Judgment* of Michael Angelo. Amongst similar work by Rubens we
may mention the *Fall of the Rebel Angels* (Munich), which is the
*St. Michael* of the letter just quoted ; the little *Last Judgment* (182 ×
120 c.m., Munich) ; the *Fall of the Damned* (286 × 224 c.m., Munich).
There are also *Judgments* at Dresden and Genoa, as well as an
*Assumption of the Just* at Munich and a *Fall of the Damned* at Aix-
la-Chapelle : two pictures already spoken of as dating from the Italian
journey.

One cannot say that Rubens has quite succeeded where his Italian
forerunners made a comparative failure. But then these vast and
complicated compositions of his were painted before he had mastered his
latest style. Rubens was slow and steady in his growth. Many
admirers have spoken of his calm mind, his deliberate thoughtfulness,
and his long and reasonable restraint of manner in painting. He always
liked exuberant composition, dramatic action, and robust forms ; but the
appearance of fury and swiftness, in his earlier pictures especially, was
not the effect of hurry or impetuousness of mind and hand. This effect
was deliberately planned, and it took Rubens years to establish a full
agreement between his handling and his composition ; the earlier, and
even a few of the later, compositions that express exuberance are painfully,

SKETCH FOR THE ASSUMPTION OF THE VIRGIN. *Albertina, Vienna.*

*From a photograph by Braun, Clément & Cie.*

almost timidly, handled. Rooses feels this in the large *Last Judgment*. Its fury looks somehow tame and frozen in spite of its dramatic gestures

*The Adoration of the Magi. Church of St. Jean, Malines.*
*From the Engraving by L. Vorsterman.*

and violent attitudes. These involved compositions have been called irreverently bunches of grapes, sacks of potatoes, bundles of sausages, etc. Yet every painter will sympathise with them as courageous studies of difficult anatomical subjects on a large scale, possibly undertaken less to satisfy an æsthetic mood than to improve, or may be to display, a knowledge of the figure.

As to the *Susanna* referred to in the Carleton list, it can hardly be identified ; Rubens made many versions of this subject from the early one at Madrid to the late version at Munich.    There exists, however, an engraving by Vorsterman of a *Susanna and the Elders*, now in Chicago Museum, which Rubens, in a letter to Peter van Veen (19th June 1622), calls one of the best reproductions of his work.    This engraving bears the following dedication to " Lectissimae Virgini Annae Roemer Visschers illustri Bataviae sijderi, multarum Artium peritissimae, Poetices vero studio, supra sexum celebri, rarum hoc Pudicitiae exemplar, Petrus Paulus Rubenus, L.M.D.D."    This lady had copied a picture by Rubens, the *Madonna squirting Milk from her Breast into the Child's Mouth.* Together with a laudatory poem on the picture, she sent a letter to Rubens asking him how he managed to grind up his white paint so that it never turned yellow.

*Achilles disguised as a Woman* was amongst the pictures refused by Carleton, and it was finally taken with others to Spain in 1628. The canvas now hangs in the Prado, where it presents, says Rooses, a perfect blending of the work of Rubens and Van Dyck into an artistic harmony of style.    *St. Peter and the Tribute Money* was probably a version of the left wing of the triptych at Notre Dame (Malines), the *Marvellous Draught of Fishes.*    This powerful, dramatic and highly-coloured picture, one of the best works of Rubens's second period, was painted in 1618-19, when the master was staying at the Château de Steen, his house in the country, not far from Malines.    A small sketch of the middle panel of this triptych, made possibly by Van Dyck for Bolswert's engraving, hangs in our National Gallery.    *Daniel in the Lions' Den* was given by Carleton to Charles I., and it finally passed into the Hamilton collection.    The lions are perhaps better than Daniel, though I judge only by the engraving.    The *Twelve Apostles and Christ,* refused by Carleton, are doubtless those now in Rome (Rospigliosi Palace).    In all but the colour, these pictures resemble the *Apostles* which Rubens left behind him in Madrid.    Probably the Roman pictures were painted by pupils from the very same drawings that Rubens had made during his first voyage to Spain in 1603-4.    To make up a

The Last Communion of St. Francis.    Antwerp Museum.
From a Photograph by Braun, Clément, & Cie.

hundred florins, still owing to Carleton on the exchange, Rubens threw in the *Hagar* of Grosvenor House, which he describes as a panel 3½ by 2½ feet in height. He says, moreover, that Hagar, though with child, quits the house with a very noble and graceful action ; he explains that he chose wood to work on, because little subjects came off better on panel than on canvas ; and he adds that he has permitted no one to touch the picture except an artist (Wildens) very talented in landscape, and that only to produce something " after your excellency's taste."

These extracts are quite sufficient to show the relations between Rubens and his pupils and collaborators ; also to explain the nature of the Antwerp picture factory which endured till the master's death.

Rooses makes the second manner of Rubens extend from about 1612 to 1625, a period which very nearly corresponds to that which I have called the quiet part of the painter's life (1609-22). The first or Italian manner was heroic, and huge in conception, yet generally hard in style, violent in chiaroscuro, and yet at times tamely academic in drawing. Its culmination is the triptych *Erection of the Cross* (1609-10), now in Antwerp Cathedral. Rooses chooses as the most prominent example of the beginning of the second manner the other triptych in Antwerp Cathedral, the *Descent from the Cross* (1612). The second manner is much more original; it started the Antwerp school, and beyond its ideal scarce any contemporary advanced. The forms are less muscular, the gestures less exaggerated, the transitions suaver, the light and shade less contrasted than in the first period, but the pigment is still solid, and the colours are treated as large, unfused blocks of decorative effect. The beauty of expressive brushwork, the parsimony of pigment, the fusion of colour which characterise the third and last manner, are not yet attained. No exact limits can be assigned to these periods, since the growth of Rubens was gradual ; but the dates given by Rooses are as right as any fixed periods could be. Amongst pictures of the second period are *St. Thomas* and the *Last Communion of St. Francis*, both in the Museum at Antwerp ; the *Adoration of the Magi* and the *Miraculous Draught of Fishes* at Malines ; the *Last Judgment* and the *Battle of the Amazons* at Munich; the *Miracles of St. Francis Xavier* and the *Miracles of St. Ignatius* at Vienna; while in England we have Lord Ashburton's *Wolf-Hunt*. Even in these pictures, especially chosen by

Max Rooses to illustrate the second manner, we can see prophecies as it were of the third, notably in the handling of the steps in the *Last Communion of St. Francis;* but if we look at other pictures, such as the *Coup de Lance,* Antwerp, an approach to the third manner is still more visible. The series of *Apostles,* that of *Decius,* that of the Jesuit Church, that of *Constantine,* that of the Luxembourg, belong to this period. It was only the organisation of the house of Rubens and Co. that enabled the master to pour out from the studio in Antwerp a steady stream of madonnas, saints, classic subjects, historical pieces, landscapes and *genre* pictures, whilst he was undertaking these huge series of palatial decorations.

Some of the portraits are very interesting and even very good, but the majority, as portraits must, lose by habit of collaboration and decorative freedom. The habit of decorative license operates two ways : first, directly, to make the painter care for style and flourish rather than likeness and construction; second, indirectly and by reaction, to make him so afraid of freedom that he becomes timid, minute, and inelegant in his workmanship. Both these moods may be seen in Rubens's portraits ; the first less decidedly pronounced than in some pictures by Titian, Lely, and many more recent painters in love with decorative style or an ideal exposition of type ; the second mood, on the other hand, never seems pushed into the minute fidelity to detail of feature and costume that characterises the work of A. Moro or the school of Bruges. No painter of courage and conscience can be found but what oscillates a little between these two attractions : style and ideality of type on one hand, construction and actuality of feature on the other. We may see this indecision in Reynolds and Gainsborough, in Whistler and Sargent, even in Velazquez himself, the first and foremost of portrait painters.

Rubens was no imitator, rather an extremely personal painter ; but the balance of his personality inclined him usually to enjoy the language of paint before the character of nature. Whether he found himself facing a human model or a painted picture he translated freely instead of copying accurately. The thing before his eyes hinted at something else in his own mind, and he pushed a type in the direction of his own taste. As he worked he fell in love with his own style, and sought to enhance the beauty of the Rubens feeling rather than to accentuate the character of

*Le Coup de Lance.   Antwerp Museum.   From a Photograph by G. Hermans.*

the beauty he was supposed to express. As you may see in London, when he copied Mantegna, it was to make an essay of his own style ; or in Madrid, when he copied Titian, it was to get a suggestion for a new Rubens. It was the man's prevailing mood to distil from any object the material of his own dreams ; yet he was so gifted that, when by a rare chance the more objective mood possessed him, he could imagine a rendering of nature that was quite sympathetic with the thing painted. One or two landscapes, one or two portraits are sufficient to prove that it was taste and not incompetence that made Rubens a conventional decorator instead of an imaginative naturalist. The landscapes *En Chasse* (Antwerp Museum), *Château de Steen*, and the smaller *Sunset* (both National Gallery) may be later than the second manner ; but we can point to such admirably natural black and white drawings as the *Kneeling Shepherdess* in the Albertina Collection, Vienna, a *Shepherdess offering an Egg* and a *Shepherdess offering a Lamb* in the same collection. The first of these drawings was done for the *Adoration of the Shepherds* at Marseilles, once on the altar of St. Jean, Malines, and the drawn figure is much finer than the painted figure. But perhaps the oil portrait *Jacqueline de Cordes* (Brussels Museum) is more proper to our purpose.

This portrait dates from 1617-18, the time of the *Miraculous Draught of Fishes* and the *Decius* series, but it is quite different in its quiet, careful execution and the sad and dignified beauty of its expression. The type, thin, slightly aquiline, and of saint-like repression, agrees little with the Rubens taste or the Rubens formula, yet the painter treats it with respect and makes no effort to force the reserved, almost ascetic, lady to become bovine and voluptuous. His swaggering brush obeys the searching, sympathetic mood of his mind, and records with honest effort his careful observation of the forms, especially those of the mouth and chin. The forehead and brows are also excellently shaped, and notably the soft and natural passage of the eyebrow on the right into its adjoining temple. This may be compared to its advantage with the corresponding part of the *Chapeau de Paille* in the National Gallery, a canvas of 1620, very lovely in colour, which, although Rooses seems to think otherwise, surely shows the hand of some one else in the comparatively rude folds of the dress, the trivial details of the feather, and the small treatment of the eyebrow. In *Jacqueline de Cordes* the hair looks timid, and the dress careful but florid like an early Velazquez ; if they are by Rubens, these details give one rather a sense of his sincerity than of his cleverness. Another picture in the Brussels Gallery persuades one more than anything that Rubens need not have altered the aspect of nature to be a great man. *Four Heads of a Negro*, or coffee-coloured Moor, are shown from different points of view and of different sizes on one canvas ; now smiling, now serious, here three-quarter face, here in profile, against a blue, loosely rubbed-in background. When you come on it in the Brussels Gallery, you experience the shock that you frequently receive from a Velazquez in the Prado, the shock that comes from being suddenly instructed by finer and keener sensations of eyesight. Much might be said about mere studies and finished decorative pictures, but this is hardly the place to say it ; one must be content to point out that this canvas shows Rubens as exact as you could wish to the shape and lighting of the thing he saw. It cannot be denied that these heads of a negro affect one much more powerfully and sympathetically than the heads of people decoratively adjusted to the feeling of a Rubens picture.

His family life, we know, greatly occupied Rubens at all times ; he had been an affectionate son and brother, he was a good husband and father. He often painted his wife and himself in his pictures, so one is not surprised that he also made direct portraits of his family. One of the earliest is the *Rubens and Isabella Brant* (Munich Gallery), painted in 1609 or 1610, when Rubens was about thirty-two and his newly-married wife little over eighteen. The figures are shown at full length but sitting, and are carefully painted in their everyday walking costumes, Rubens wearing a kind of tall hat. Later comes the *Isabella Brant* of Windsor Castle and the drawing in the National Gallery, both about 1614. As she gets older we see her in the picture at the Hague (1620), and finally in that of the Hermitage Gallery, St. Petersburg (1625). There are others at Florence and in the collections of the Duke of Norfolk and the late Sir Richard Wallace. The sons of Rubens by Isabella Brant, Albert (1614-57) and Nicholas (1618-55), appear together in a picture at the Liechtenstein Gallery, Vienna, painted about 1625 ; while of Nicholas alone at the age of two there is a portrait in the Berlin Museum. The *Chapeau de Paille* in the National Gallery has already been mentioned ; it depicts Susan Fourment (1599-1643), one of the many

*The Emperor Theodosius repulsed by St. Ambrose from the door of Milan Cathedral.*
*Imperial Gallery, Vienna. From a Photograph by Lötvy.*

daughters of Daniel Fourment and successively wife of Raymond del Monte and Arnold Lunden. She used to be called the mistress of Rubens, but apparently for no better reason than that a lady of the kind was considered a necessary encumbrance even for a painter so married as Rubens. Other paintings and drawings of her by Rubens exist, and also one picture at St. Petersburg, supposed to be done by Van Dyck.

Rubens was an admirable draughtsman, and the character of his work with the point is often more realistic and natural than that of his painted decorations. It is impossible in a mere sketch like the present to speak adequately of the large collections of Rubens's drawings at Vienna, Paris, London, and elsewhere. The drawings in the Albertina collection, Vienna, which he made with his own hand for the *Defeat of Sennacherib* (Munich), seem in advance of the picture, a work of the year 1614. They are very lightly touched monochromes, made either for the engravers who were to reproduce, or for the pupils who were to lay in, the picture. A wonderful sentiment of movement and agitation is expressed in the slightest of these with very little material. The angel leaning from the thunderous sky and the majestic horses rearing with fury and terror are scarcely indicated, and yet no elaboration could add to the feeling of excited motion. In portraiture, too, the drawings often appear more spirited and more individual than the pictures. Whether like the models or not, no drawings could give one a more lively sense of personality than those of the *Duke of Buckingham* (1625), *Peter Paul Rubens* (1628), a *Maid of Honour of the Archduchess Isabella, Two Girls' Heads*, and the *Marie de Medicis* (1622), all at Vienna. The pen-and-ink drawing, *Assumption of the Virgin*, connected with no special painted version of the subject, and the chalk drawing for the *Martyrdom of St. Catherine* (Lille, 1622 *circa*), both come from the Albertina Collection. The drawing from the Louvre, which was the first idea for the *Elevation of the Cross*, differs in many respects from the picture. In the drawing the cross leans to the soldiers and away from the Virgin, but Rubens reversed its inclination in the picture. Less traditional and more personal are the two beautifully expressive drawings of a *Boar's Head*, one seen full face, the other in profile. They come from the British Museum, as does the elegant *Hunting Scene*.

# CHAPTER III

*The Medicis and Constantine series—Visits to Paris and Holland—The series of the
triumphs of the Faith—The political missions of Rubens—Spain and England—
His second marriage—Missions to Holland.*

THE date and subject of the drawing of Marie de Medicis bring us
to a time of change in the even tenor of Rubens's life. In January
1622 Rubens started for Paris, summoned by Marie de Medicis, who
at last found leisure to think of the decoration of her favourite Luxembourg Palace. The Queen-Mother of France, even if she had not
remarked Rubens at her wedding in Florence, knew him now by
his European reputation, by the notorious favour of his own sovereigns,
by the report of her sister the Duchess of Mantua, by the recollections
of her own portrait-painter, F. Pourbus, once associated with Rubens
at the court of Mantua, and by the warm recommendation of the Flemish
ambassador, Baron de Vicq. At Paris Rubens saw a great deal of
Nicholas Peiresc, a learned man to whom he had been introduced by
Gevartius. Peiresc was much pleased with Rubens, and from that time
took a warm interest in his work. Many were the letters which passed
between them concerning the pictures of the Luxembourg series and
those of the series treating the life of the Emperor Constantine the
Great. The Constantine series was a commission from Louis XIII., and
the pictures were cartoons meant to be used for tapestry. Thus upon
the top of the large order for the Jesuit church in Antwerp, Rubens
accepted two others, one from Louis XIII. and the other from the Queen-
Mother. The painter stayed a month or two in Paris, and arranged to
do the decoration of the Luxembourg for 20,000 écus ; by 4th March
he was back at Antwerp with measurements and drawings of the principal
personages. By the end of 1622 several of the Constantine cartoons had

The Infant Jesus, St. John, and two Angels. Berlin Gallery. From a Photograph by F. Hanfstaengl.

reached Paris, and had been seen by Peiresc and other connoisseurs. In December 1622 Peiresc writes an interesting letter to Rubens full of praise, yet not without a little timid advice and even gentle criticism. He tells his friend that besides many enthusiastic admirers of the cartoons there were a few daring and envious critics who carped at small faults. "Every one, however, was obliged to confess that no French artist could hope to become able to create such a work as this although it was executed by the hands of your pupils ; that, in fact, they were looking at the creation of a great man and a lofty genius." Peiresc also alludes to Rubens's manner of arching legs instead of drawing them straight, *selon l'usage*. While he remembers what Rubens had told him of the fine curvature of the legs in the Florentine *Moses*, in the *St. Paul*, and in many instances from actual nature, nevertheless he begs his friend not to go against Raphael, M. Angelo, Correggio, and the Greeks, and not to shock the weak minds of fashionable people enslaved to tradition. He criticises the drawing of the thighs of two men hanging from the bridge in the *Defeat of Maxentius*, and implores Rubens to correct the mistake with his own hand.

When he returned to Paris, Rubens brought with him the smaller canvases of the Medicis series, completely finished. The two large chimney-piece decorations (727 × 394 c.m.) he painted on the spot, and during this work he saw a great deal of the Queen-Mother. He was treated with affability, and Marie de Medicis talked freely with him, asking his opinion on the beauty of the ladies of her court. He gave the preference to the celebrated beauty, Madame de Guémenée. Rubens painted several portraits at this time ; amongst others, one of the Duke of Buckingham, one of the Baron de Vicq, and one of the Baroness, his wife. But in spite of this fine reception and notable favour, Rubens found no small difficulty and delay in getting the money for his Luxembourg decorations. In December 1625 he writes to Peiresc complaining of the expenses he had incurred in his work and in his journeys, and declares that he counts the whole business a loss, but for the generosity of the Duke of Buckingham, whom he had met in Paris.

About this time, probably on his return to Antwerp from Paris, he painted *Ambrogio Spinola*, afterwards celebrated by Velazquez in the *Surrender of Breda*. Spinola had become the minister and counsellor of the Archduchess, and very much favoured the employment of

*The Archduke Albert.   Brussels Museum.*
*From a Photograph by F. Hanfstaengl.*

Rubens in political affairs.   The painter's inclination to occupy himself
with matters that kept him active was increased by the death of his

wife, Isabella Brant, in June 1626.   To divert his mind from this sorrow, he was easily persuaded, in 1627, to pay his third visit to Holland,

*The Archduchess Isabella.   Brussels Museum.*
*From a Photograph by F. Hanfstengl.*

when he had for companion, during a great part of the time, the painter and writer Joachim Sandrart.   He saw many artists, he bought some pictures, and, during the long journeys in post-chaises, he held those conversations on art which Sandrart reported in his *Academia Tedesca*.

Rubens and his school were also occupied, in 1627, on a series of designs for tapestry, to the order of the Archduchess Isabella, who wished to present hangings to her own Convent of Cordelière nuns at Madrid. The subjects were taken from the mysteries of the Faith, and particularly illustrated the triumphs of the Eucharist over Heresy, Philosophy, Science, Idolatry, Ignorance, and other spiritual enemies. It was, indeed, a subject well suited to the recipients, and to their surroundings, though hardly, one would think, agreeable to the secret views of the painter. The Fitzwilliam Museum, Cambridge, possesses some sketches of the principal pictures, and some of the canvases themselves may be seen in the Louvre, in the Prado, and especially in Grosvenor House, London, belonging to the Duke of Westminster.

In 1623 the political life of Rubens began to assume importance, and his work on these large decorations was interrupted by a mission to Holland. The Archduke Albert's death in 1621 may have caused the Archduchess Isabella and her minister to take Rubens into their inner counsels, and to employ him in semi-official missions to foreign courts. Painters were political agents, who could be used to convey instructions, or to sound important personages, without giving the little diplomatic movement all the publicity and the importance of an embassy. Although it is impossible to go fully into the history of the day, a word on political affairs in general will not be out of place. Spain was declining in power; as he refused to believe this, James I. of England wished for a Spanish alliance, a mistaken policy, which his son, Charles I., was inclined to follow. Richelieu, a much further seeing politician than any man of his time, knew that the day of Spain was over, and set little store by her friendship and support. The Emperor of Austria soon became occupied with the Thirty Years' War, and unable to aid Spain. Therefore one of the objects of the Spanish rulers of Flanders was to keep England friendly with Spain, and apart from France. Another was to be at peace with Holland; the treaty with Holland expired at the Archduke Albert's death, and it was to arrange for its renewal that Rubens went to the Hague in 1623. Indeed, either Holland or England was the cause of all the political undertakings in which Rubens

A MAID OF HONOUR OF THE ARCHDUCHESS ISABELLA. *Albertina, Vienna.*

*From a photograph by Braun, Clément & Cie.*

was employed. His first mission to Holland had little result, except, perhaps, the advancement of the painter himself. It was found that a mere burgess was inapt for kingly counsels and political missions. So he was ennobled by the King of Spain, which means, I suppose, that he became an *armiger,* or one who had the right to bear arms.

In the mess of politics which involved Rubens from 1623 to 1633 Balthazar Gerbier (1592-1667, afterwards knighted by Charles I.) played an important if not a very straightforward part. Gerbier was born of a French father who had left his country at the Massacre of St. Bartholomew ; like other men educated as painters, he became a traveller, adviser, and dealer for the great men who collected works of art, and from this position he passed naturally into the convenient and more remunerative business of political agent, news-retailer, and secret spy. When the Autotype Company first published it, W. E. Henley showed me a Gerbier from the picture by Van Dyck, and said, "If you don't know this man, tell me what you think of him." I replied, "A detected skunk about to be kicked for some mean business." Indeed, the face is stamped with an expression compounded of fear, anger, and false cunning. Gerbier worked for Charles I. and for Buckingham, whom he accompanied to Spain in 1623. He had a house and family in England, but he was often abroad, and during the period of Rubens's political activity Gerbier was frequently at his side sharing in his travels, leading him on to speak, and reporting everything to the English court.

Buckingham was hated by Richelieu in France and Olivarez in Spain, so that Rubens and his employers had a complicated business to manage when they would push England and Spain into each other's arms. Buckingham had been very friendly to Rubens in that noble and generous way of his which Dumas exaggerates so delightfully in the *Musketeers.* Both in Paris, when Rubens made a drawing of the Duke which rivals Dumas's description for distinguished and chivalrous beauty, and in Antwerp, when Buckingham visited, admired, and finally purchased the Rubens collection, the painter and the minister seemed to approach an agreement on the advantages of an English-Spanish friendship. But in haughty resentment against the Richelieu who had separated him from Anne of Austria, Buckingham took up the cause of the Huguenots of La Rochelle ; of course Rubens failed to induce Spain to follow the

E

Duke into such a war and into the company of such allies. Gerbier, taking the cue from his master, gave Rubens the cold shoulder, and would scarcely answer the letters which Rubens continued to write at the request of the Archduchess and Spinola.

At last, after some shilly-shally, the rulers of Flanders determined to send Rubens to the court of Philip IV. to discover the true feelings of the King ; moreover, at the same moment, Buckingham began to come round, and on 4th April 1628 himself proposed the mission of Rubens to Spain. Towards the end of this summer Rubens set out on his second voyage to that country, taking with him eight pictures as a present to Philip, a real lover of art, not merely a prince who thought painting a luxury necessary to his position. The death of Buckingham on the 2nd of September, and the capture of La Rochelle by Richelieu, allowed Rubens to turn from politics to art and to live in the society of the only man who could admire him without forgetting his own view of beauty and truth.

Rubens, now fifty-two, and Velazquez thirty, painted together, travelled together, and talked together for eight or nine months. In the presence of Velazquez, Rubens copied Titian ; retouched old pictures by himself, such as an *Adoration of the Magi*, originally painted in 1610 ; and also made new ones, amongst which, according to Pacheco, the father-in-law of Velazquez, were many portraits of the Royal Family, and five of the King himself. This was the special province of Velazquez, but he does not seem to have been jealous or to have resented the repeated orders for pictures sent to Rubens from this time up to the day of his death. Pacheco says that Rubens was best pleased when he was in the company of Velazquez, and that he conceived a high esteem for the younger man's talents as a painter. The two made several expeditions together ; on one occasion they climbed the Sierras to take bird's-eye-view sketches of the Escorial  Can this illustrious commerce of the two great geniuses who represented realistic and decorative painting have been without influence on the younger ?  Not only had Rubens more than twenty years' start in the race, but Velazquez progressed slowly as all realists, while Rubens in intention, at least, was himself even during his first voyage to Spain. Rubens's brush, it is true, became more supple with experience, and when he knew Velazquez he had gained the

*The Education of the Virgin.    Antwerp Museum.*
*From a Photograph by Braun, Clément, & Cie.*

entrancing freedom of touch, the variegated richness of harmony in colour, and the full command of a most sweet and fluent vehicle. Velazquez, on the contrary, had painted up to this moment in a somewhat hard and dense medium. *The Topers*, on which he was then occupied, in spite of its originality and vigour, still looks a little hard and metallic. Velazquez must have studied Philip's fine collection of Italian pictures, but he had an eye of his own for nature that could not be denied or deceived. Not even the most seductive eloquence of the Italian style had been able to persuade him to forget the more sympathetic voice of nature. At the age of thirty Rubens had been seven years in Italy, and was meditating new visions of decorative art ; at thirty here was Velazquez still absorbed in the translation of his own eyesight, and for the first time in his life speaking on painting with a man of his own powers, though of ten times his reputation. Up to twenty-nine one cannot say that Velazquez had pursued style or cultivated decorative effect ; but from the first he had possessed a closer appreciation of form than Rubens ever attained. Rubens was accustomed to teaching ; could he have refrained from giving counsel when he met a young man even more gifted than his favourite Van Dyck? At least, may he not have whispered something of a pleasanter brown, a more winning and more delicate use of pigment? Rubens would not be altogether astonished at Velazquez ; he would not value his sincerity and his insight when they differed from his own, while he could not help knowing that he himself was a much more accomplished painter than this violent demonstrator of the natural and the ugly, who had not covered churches and palaces with surprising and coherent fantasies. But Velazquez would admire Rubens without reserve ; his work was no more unnatural than any other man's, while it was plainly expert and splendidly imaginative. One thing is certain, Rubens told the young man that he needed experience, the study of beautiful art, and the society of Italian masters. He went further ; he persuaded Philip IV. to send Velazquez to Italy.

It is impossible in so short a life of Rubens to go through the long list of pictures that he painted in Spain. Villaamil says that had he tied himself closely down to painting during his whole stay, each canvas would have taken on the average seven days' work. But in reality it took much less time ; for the painter rode, hunted, travelled, paid visits, and wrote letters. One of his letters from Spain to his friend Gevartius is quoted by Michiels to show that Rubens, if religious in his heart, was by no means a bigot or an extreme believer in the authority of a Church. The painter, in case he should die, asks Gevartius to look after his son and to educate him rather in his museum than in his oratory. This alone means little, and even if we add to it other signs of enlightenment, we may not say that Rubens's outward conformity was merely the politic fraud of an ambitious man. He may have believed in the general efficacy of the Christian faith without believing in the bigoted and cruel government of the Church or in the violent and quarrelsome self-sufficiency of the schismatics. At any rate, he did not wish his son to grow up priest-ridden or a slave to ritual.

Friendship between Spain and England now became possible, and Philip agreed that Rubens should directly represent him on a more or less open visit to Charles I. An English vessel conveyed the painter and his brother-in-law, Henry Brant, to England, where they were lodged by the King's order, and at his expense, in the house of Balthazar Gerbier. The painter reached London on the 25th May, and remained in the country about eight months, during which time he visited the provinces, and amongst other places Cambridge, where he and his friends received honorary degrees from the University. Whilst he was duly sounding the King's mind, to measure his desire for a peace with Spain, Rubens also held conversations with Charles on the subject of painting. The first Rubens which the King had owned was a *Judith and Holophernes*, bought when he was Prince of Wales. Concerning this picture, one of the Prince's advisers on art, Lord Danvers, afterwards Earl of Danby, writes on 27th March 1621 : "But now for Rubens ; in every paynter's opinion he hath sent hether a peece scarse touched by his own hand, and the postures so forced, as the prince will not admit the picture into his galerye. I could wishe, thearfore, that this famus man would doe soum thinge to register or redeem his reputation in this howse and to stand amongst the many excelent wourkes which are hear of all the best masters in Christendoum, for from him we have yet only *Judeth and Holifernes* of littel credit to his great skill." Now here are Rubens's own words on the picture, written in a letter to William Trumbull, September 1621 : " Je seray bien ayse que ceste

THE DUKE OF BUCKINGHAM. *Albertina, Vienna.*

*From a photograph by Braun, Clément & Cie.*

pièce soit colloqué en un lieu si éminent comme la galerie de S. A. Monsr. le Prince de Galles et feray tout mon extrême debvoir afin de

*Rubens, drawn by himself. Albertina, Vienna.*
*From a Photograph by Braun, Clément, & Cie.*

la rendre supérieure d'artifice à celle d'Holofernes laquelle j'ay fait en ma jeunesse." Ruelens speaks of a *Judith and Holophernes* belonging to Madame Brun at Carpentras as *fin* in workmanship, *mais dur de ton*. He is not sure whether it is a copy or an original of the early period. Rooses remarks on its agreement with the engraving, by Cornelius Galle, called *La Grande Judith*. This print is burdened with folds and details, which may be over-emphasised by the engraver, but certainly the main shapes of the composition are stately and Rubens-like. It was about 1624 that the superb portrait of Rubens at Windsor [1] was acquired, as may be seen from these words in a letter written on the 1st of March 1623 by W. Trumbull to Sir Dudley Carleton : " My Lord Danvers desyreing nowe to have his *Creation* of Bassano againe because Rubens hath mended it very well, doth by a lettre commande me to treate with him, for his owne pourtrait to be placed in the Prince's gallery." Rubens, while he complied, protested that he did not think it good manners to send his own portrait to a prince of such high degree. Reproductions of this picture abound, also replicas, but the engraving by Pontius is perhaps the most known.

Charles I. had intended for some time to carry out his father's wish to decorate the ceiling of the banqueting saloon at Whitehall. He now entrusted the work to Rubens, who, with the series of Henry IV. still unfinished, many smaller works on hand, and so much political travelling, must have been considerably in arrears and altogether overwhelmed with commissions. But Rubens, as he was not in Antwerp directing affairs, found time to paint a few extra pictures in England. Amongst other things he did the *Gerbier Family*, a portrait of *Old Parr*, and *Peace and War* (National Gallery). On 21st February 1830, before Rubens left England, Charles knighted the painter and sent him to Flanders with an increased reputation, a gold chain and hopes of peace with Spain.

After a short visit at the court of Philip IV. to render an account of his mission, Rubens again began work at Antwerp. He had the *Henry IV.* series on his hands, the *Achilles* series to finish, and the Whitehall decorations to begin. The *Henry IV.* series he never completed ; Marie de Medicis was exiled in 1831, and letters in the Sainsbury papers show that when she came to Antwerp, Rubens was rather employed in raising money for her than in receiving it himself.

[1] Reproduced in the *Portfolio* monograph on the *Picture Gallery of Charles I.*

*Rubens and his second Wife, Hélène Fourment, in a Garden. Pinakotck, Munick.*

*From a Photograph by F. Hanfstaengl.*

Isabella Brant had now been dead about four years ; Rubens was not the man to settle down alone in an empty house, and on the 6th December 1630 he married Helen Fourment. Her appearance pleased Rubens ; indeed, women of her type had always haunted the painter's canvases, and now from this time she herself, the incarnation of the Rubens ideal of Venus, sat for many of the personages in her husband's pictures. Helen was the youngest of the seven daughters of Daniel Fourment, and Rubens must have known her from her childhood, since Isabella Brant's sister Clara was the second wife of Daniel Fourment. Indeed he often painted her brothers and sisters long before 1830, as witness the *Chapeau de Paille*, a portrait of her sister Susan Fourment. Helen was born the same year, 1614, as Rubens's eldest son Albert, so that she was a girl of sixteen when she married this old gentleman of fifty-three, who suffered from the gout, but was famous and very handsome, a noble and fairly rich. There are many portraits of Helen Fourment besides those pictures in which she is introduced under another character. One of these, at Munich, shows Helen Fourment and Rubens with a boy walking in their garden whilst an old servant feeds the fowls. The superb full-length *Hélène Fourment à la Pelisse* at Vienna gives a portrait of Helen wrapped only in a fur-bordered cloak, which heightens the effect of her dazzling skin. There are also excellent portraits at the Louvre, the Hague, St Petersburg, and elsewhere. In the case of many portraits painted after 1624, unless there happens to be documentary evidence, it becomes extremely difficult to settle the date only by the mere appearance of the person. For instance, Rooses gives the date 1625-26 to the *Albert and Nicholas* of the Liechtenstein Gallery, Vienna, judging by apparent ages of the sitters ; but Mr Claude Phillips maintains, on the strength of his resemblance to Helen, that the younger boy is not Nicholas, son of the first wife, but Francis Rubens (1633-78), son of the second wife, which, if true, would assign the picture to the last years of Rubens's life.

Although Rubens very soon after his marriage fell again into the political whirlpool, still he never left off painting, and he seems to have kept up his interest in all matters concerning art and learning. On 1st August 1631 he wrote a very interesting letter to Junius, the Earl of Arundel's librarian, who had written a book on *The Painting of the Ancients*.

Although he praises the book warmly he takes occasion to put forth the painter's perpetual plea that in painting the eye is more concerned than the ear; but how gravely and mildly he states his point! One hardly feels the full import of the words unless one is familiar with the sentiment. The tenor of the letter runs : God forbid that I should level myself with the Ancients or fail in respect to their work ; but we cannot see a picture described by Pliny or the expression of Eurydice's face in a lost composition, whereas we can still buy and still admire Italian works of art. He hints that the scholarship of art which treats at length of what neither the writer nor the reader may ever see were better devoted to matters that may be still judged with feeling and with critical inquiry. The letter bears a postscript saying that Rubens wrote it standing on one leg ; we may therefore assume that his life was not leisurely at this moment. He was soon busy over the question of the Dutch Treaty, meeting at Dunkirk the Marquis d'Aytona who had succeeded the deceased Spinola, running here and there to confer with deputies at Liège or to visit politicians in Holland, but ever spied upon by the watchful and furtive Gerbier, who complains, in letters to Charles I. and Lord Dorchester, that it is difficult to draw the painter on the subject of his political intentions. Twice at least Rubens went to the Prince of Orange, and the second time he was ill received and even threatened with arrest. In fact his efforts led to very little result except a final humiliation at the beginning of 1633, which inclined him to dislike the business of political agent. On his return from the Hague the Duke of Aerschot, one of the popular leaders, demanded an account of his mission and insisted on seeing his papers. Rubens, strong in the orders of Isabella, absolutely refused to show them or to call on the Duke. Letters passed between them, firm on the part of the painter, haughty and peremptory on the part of the great man ; who ended up with " Je seray bien aise que vous appreniez dorénavant comme doivent escrire à des gens de ma sorte ceux de la vostre." Rubens apologised, perhaps too humbly, and the Duke went about showing the correspondence in triumph. Writers have loaded the Duke with abuse for his share in this business, but something may be said for him and the Deputies to the States-General whom he represented. They were the patriotic party, desirous of more power in the management of affairs, and they regarded

*Hélène Fourment. Hermitage, St. Petersburg.*
*From a Photograph by Braun, Clément, & Cie.*

Rubens as a Spanish agent, the friend of tyranny, and not as one eager to do good to his country.

The death of his friend and patron the Archduchess Isabella in 1633 determined the disgusted Rubens to abandon politics, which he had better have left alone from the first. Ambition, a taste for grandeur, the force of circumstances, the importunity of others, gradually led Rubens into this worrying and treacherous life, which laid him open to the insolence of officials and superiors. In those days, doubtless, it was better either to remain very obscure or to become very powerful, since such a successful man as Rubens, at the height of his fame, could be bullied and humiliated by a Grand Seigneur. Perhaps Artus, the Dutch painter of Leyden, in the century before, chose the better part in wishing to remain entirely unknown. Michiels says that the renowned Franz Floris visited him and offered to take him to Antwerp, introduce him to the world, and enable him to live like a lord. Artus told Floris that he had no desire for luxury, that he had no envy of the great, that he limited his desires to living gaily and peacefully in his broken-down old shanty of a house.

# CHAPTER IV

*Last Years of Rubens's Life and Work*

INCREASING gout caused Rubens to live so quietly in the following years that he was not even able to be present at the great event of the time —the entry into Antwerp of Ferdinand, the brother of Philip IV. Ferdinand succeeded Isabella in the viceroyalty of Flanders, and he made his triumphal entry into Antwerp in 1635 after travels, delays, and even a battle on the way. It was Rubens who had charge of the decorations and the triumphal arches, and, with some depression, he must have thought of the time when he helped Vaenius with the preparations for the entry of his own familiar sovereigns, Albert and Isabella. Two of his designs for arches and one of a triumphal car may be seen painted on panels in the Antwerp Museum. They are very slight, free and elegant, evidently quite his own work—a thin brown wash dexterously touched with solider modelling of the brighter parts. Gevartius, as secretary to the Town Council, wrote an account of these celebrations ; Van Thulden, one of Rubens's good pupils, undertook the illustrations, with the exception of two by the master himself, one a frontispiece, the drawing of which is still preserved in the Fitzwilliam Museum, Cambridge ; the other an equestrian portrait of Ferdinand. For the drawing of the triumphal car Rubens received from the town of Antwerp 84 florins worth of *vin de Paris*. The painter's favour at court, and his political missions in the interest of Spain, caused certain people to regard him as a time-server, one careless of true patriotism and tepid in the popular cause. Rooses thinks that his decoration, *Commerce quitting Antwerp*, set up during the " solemn entry," may be taken as a kind of secret protest against the mistakes of the Spanish

*Henry IV. receiving the Portrait of Marie de Medicis. Louvre.*
*From a Photograph by Neurdein.*

Government. The galleries of Vienna and Dresden possess large pictures also painted for this public festival, that of Brussels the portraits of Albert and Isabella, which are excellently reproduced in these pages.

About this date, 1635, Rubens sent to England the pictures that now adorn the ceiling of Whitehall. To save the heavy duty they were embarked at Dunkirk, which was still an English port. When they arrived at London it was found that Rubens had miscalculated the English foot, and the canvases never properly fitted their places. Subsequent damp and unskilful restoration have still further damaged the paintings ; but, in spite of cutting, mildewing, and repainting, one is forced to admit that the general aspect of the decorations is very noble, and very suitable to the size and height of the hall. Both this and the Medicis series have been abused for the mixture of fable and history, mythology and real life, which enters into their composition. Still they are full of beauties, and, where it can be easily seen, as in the Medicis series, admirably true and dignified gesture. Every one must remember the stately figures in the *Landing of Marie de Medicis ;* the grace of the bowing courtier, the haughty air of the Queen, and the rich and splendid pomp of the surroundings ; the golden barge, the green water lashed up by exuberant creatures of the stream, Neptune and the buxom wallowing nymphs of the Rhone. Our idea of Henry IV. is tied to that splendid idealisation, that fusion of king, lover, and romantic adventurer which came so naturally from the creative brush of Rubens, and which is very well shown in the picture *Henry IV. receiving the Portrait of Marie de Medicis.* It was only when he sat down before a little canvas to make a common likeness of a common human being that Rubens's inspiration sometimes failed him. On the tide of conception which bore him through a great work, Rubens was often both natural and imaginative, portrait-painter and decorator. As Mr. Henley says of Burns, to see him at his best you must see him stimulated by the romantic touch of his predecessors. In Rubens's case emulation of the great Italian decorators warmed him to his work, and a portrait tuned to the key of a decorative picture has often more seeming vitality and character than a direct likeness taken deliberately from the sitter.

Rubens was not paid more quickly by Charles than by Marie de Medicis, and Gerbier wrote letters to the King complaining that people talked of his royal master's poverty or penury with unbecoming freedom. Indeed Rubens may at times have felt pinched by a want of ready money ; he bought many pictures and curios, and his expenses were great in every direction. One must not build much, however, on his selling the choice of his Italian treasures to the Duke of Buckingham ; for political ends he may have wished to conciliate that nobleman. Even if he wanted money occasionally, as one might think from a letter in which he complains to Peiresc that he is out of pocket over the Medicis series, he could never be really distressed, since his picture-factory was always running at Antwerp, and year by year he was turning out easel-pictures by himself or his pupils. During this last period of his life, from 1630 to 1640, he put forth a great deal of very fine work, in spite of his growing tendency to gout. Philip IV. was a constant customer of these later years, and through his brother Ferdinand he ordered many pictures from Rubens and his pupils. Moreover, the King employed Rubens as a kind of agent or buyer of works of art, so that not all the pictures sent to Spain by Rubens during these years were by his own hand, or even by those of his pupils.

Between 1630 and 1636 Rubens sent twenty-five pictures to Philip's first Queen, Isabella de Bourbon ; but the King was so pleased with them that he put them in his supper-room next his own bedroom. In 1636 Philip, through his brother, ordered more pictures to decorate the Torre de la Parada, a hunting lodge, some miles from Madrid. At the end of 1637 they were not ready, and, according to Ferdinand's letters, Rubens would fix no precise date, but only promised that he and the other painters would not lose an hour of daylight. On the 21st of January 1638 Rubens wanted still twenty days more to allow the canvases time to dry properly ; and the Cardinal Archduke wisely agreed, remarking to Philip, " Comme il s'y entend mieux que moi, j'ai cédé." Buyers of to-day might take a lesson from the modesty of this royal patron of the arts. On the 11th March 1638 the pictures left for Spain, and amongst them were the *Battle of the Lapiths and Centaurs,* the *Rape of Proserpine, Orpheus and Eurydice,* the *Banquet of Tereus,* and one or two others, as well as much work by pupils and friends. Probably *Juno creating the Milky Way, Vulcan, Mercury and Argus, Fortune, Flora,* and others by Rubens or his school were amongst the

*The Martyrdom of St. Liévin.   Brussels Museum.*
*From the Engraving by Caukercken.*

numbers that swelled this huge list of 1638 to the total of 112 pictures. Most of them were destined for the decoration of the Palace of Buen Retiro, to which Velazquez also contributed no small amount of work, and amongst other things his famous *Surrender of Breda.* No sooner was this vast cargo arrived in Spain than Philip sent a fresh order for more pictures to be despatched with all expedition. They were sent off on 27th February 1639. Ferdinand, in his letter to the King, says that Rubens, "to gain time," was obliged to do them all with his own hand. This supports the legend of his wonderful rapidity of execution ; his pictures were not finished the faster for collaboration, but by its aid he could undertake several large commissions at the same time. The *Judgment of Paris,* now in the Prado, the latest and finest of his three versions of this subject, belongs to this period of his life and to the same year, 1639, as the *Three Graces* of the Prado. They are notably characteristic of the late Rubens working on secular subjects which gave a free scope to his exuberant and joyous temperament. Age, illness, sorrow, and political distraction had enfeebled his body, but they were unable to tame the rich sensuousness of his conception. Never did Rubens show his intense appreciation of the beauty of flesh and the delights of colour more conspicuously than in the pictures of his old age. The two pictures in the Prado just mentioned contain, if I remember rightly, life-sized nudes painted with such an admirable gusto that even the votary of slender forms is almost persuaded to renounce his natural worship. The figures in the *Judgment of Paris* (National Gallery) are much below life-size, and, although almost entirely the work of Rubens, represent him in a more chastened mood than that which inspired the *Three Graces* of the Prado. His *Three Graces* of the Uffizi, Florence, may please some by their slenderer and more Italian stateliness, but they please certain minds simply because they are not an expression of the real Rubens. The function of imagination in painting mainly regulates the artist's relation to nature, and only to a minor extent his adaptation of older pictorial formulas and traditions. Imagination is shown in the way a painter grapples with his own view of facts, and, as it were, forces nature to assist him in expressing his emotions about the world of forms, colours, and lights. People are apt to call a painter imaginative in proportion as he copies the style of old pictures, whose aspect has become for us a sign of poetical and religious feeling. To follow the things that Raphael liked in the world, or the types and methods of a still older art, is to play with other men's imaginations in a decorative or dilettante spirit instead of creating new types and new visions out of the raw material of one's own tastes and tendencies. In fact it is culture, taste at the best, and never imagination ; the studious intelligence of the man who sees through the eyes of the early Italians or the later Rossetti ; not the first-hand conception of those who make new art, as Rembrandt, Velazquez, Manet, Corot, and, in one half of his work, Rubens. Such considerations, however, belong more properly to an essay on the art of Rubens than to a short life in which one has not space to treat them at sufficient length, or to reconcile them with former statements on portraiture.

Further commissions from Philip found Rubens suffering under attacks of the gout, which obliged him to intermit his painting with periods of idleness. Some of these pictures were to be done in collaboration with Snyders, others by Rubens alone. Four large canvases, *Hercules, Andromeda*, a *Reconciliation of the Romans and Sabines*, and a *Rape of the Sabines*, were to be painted entirely by the master. Before his death, in May 1640, Rubens had only finished one of these four, and had merely laid in the others. Ferdinand turned to Van Dyck, who had just left England, as the best person to finish them, but he refused the job, and offered a work of his own to supply the place of one of the four. But Van Dyck also had no more time to work ; although twenty-two years younger than Rubens, he only survived his master a few months, and died in December 1641. To Jordaens, then, the heirs of Rubens allotted the task of completing two of the pictures, which the master had left unfinished — an ungrateful and an unnecessary task, which in almost every case were better left undone. The King of Spain was not the only buyer who waited for his purchases till Rubens was dead. In 1637, Jabach, a banker, a collector, and a dealer of some renown, had ordered, through the Dutch painter Gueldorp, an altar-piece from Rubens for the Cathedral of Cologne. Rubens accepted willingly, and in writing he mentions his " affection for the town where he had been brought up till he was ten years old." The *Martyrdom of St. Peter*, which he painted for this commission, did not reach Cologne till after Rubens was dead and buried.

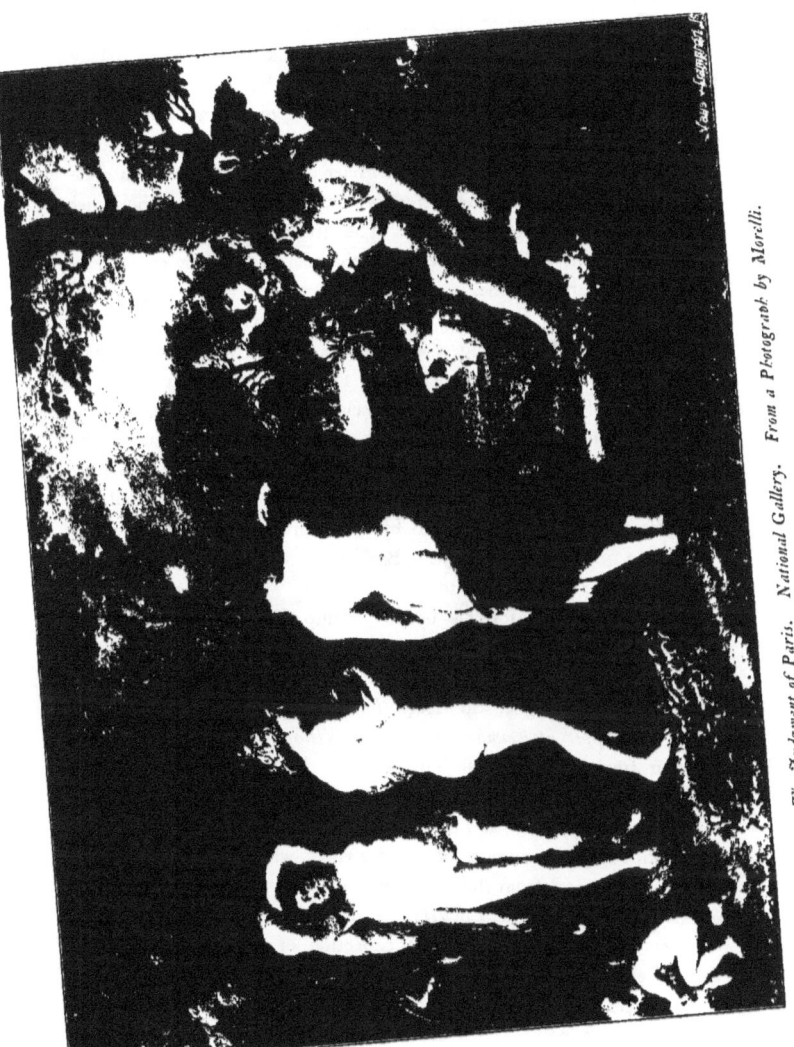

*The Judgment of Paris. National Gallery. From a Photograph by Morelli.*

This Jabach was one of those into whose hands fell some of the vast collection of works of art which Rubens left behind at his death. Many of these consisted of paintings and drawings by his own hand ; many, again, were the works of other men that he had accumulated in the course of his life. By his will Rubens left family portraits and such-like to his own wife and children ; to Helen Fourment, for instance, he specially bequeathed the *Hélène Fourment à la Pelisse*, which shows her in a somewhat undressed condition. The drawings were to be sold for the benefit of his heirs, together with the pictures, except copies and works by other artists, which were to be reserved till his youngest child should reach eighteen, in case any of them might become painters or might marry a painter. The youngest was Constance Albertina, who was born on 3rd February 1641, after her father's death, and became a nun in the Convent of La Cambre, near Brussels. Albert, the eldest, a quiet, studious person, died of grief in 1657 at the death of his son by the bite of a mad dog; Nicholas died before him in 1655 ; of Helen's children, the eldest, Clara, died in 1689, Francis in 1678, Isabella in 1652, Peter Paul in 1684. As to Helen Fourment, she married again, and made a good match with Jean Baptiste Broeckhoven, a chevalier, a baron, a count, and an ambassador.

Ferdinand, acting for his brother Philip IV., bought thirty-two pictures, eighteen of which were by Rubens, for the sum of 27,100 florins. Several of those by Rubens still exist in Madrid, as *St. George and the Dragon*, the *Holy Family and Saints*, *Nymphs and Satyrs*, the *Supper at Emmaus*, a *Dance of Villagers* ; also several copies or rather free translations of Titians which Rubens had made during his second sojourn in Spain ; one of these, *Adam and Eve* in the Prado, may still be compared with Titian's original in the same gallery.

Jabach secured a number of the drawings, which he afterwards sold to Louis XIV., and from the royal collection they have passed into the national museum of the Louvre. Vienna, as we have already said, possesses the largest and the best collection of drawings by Rubens. Most of the sketches in monochrome, and many of the drawings made for engravers, are less certainly by Rubens than the studies made from nature which afterwards served for pictures. The appearance of Rubens when old may be seen in the *Virgin with Saints* of the St. Jacques

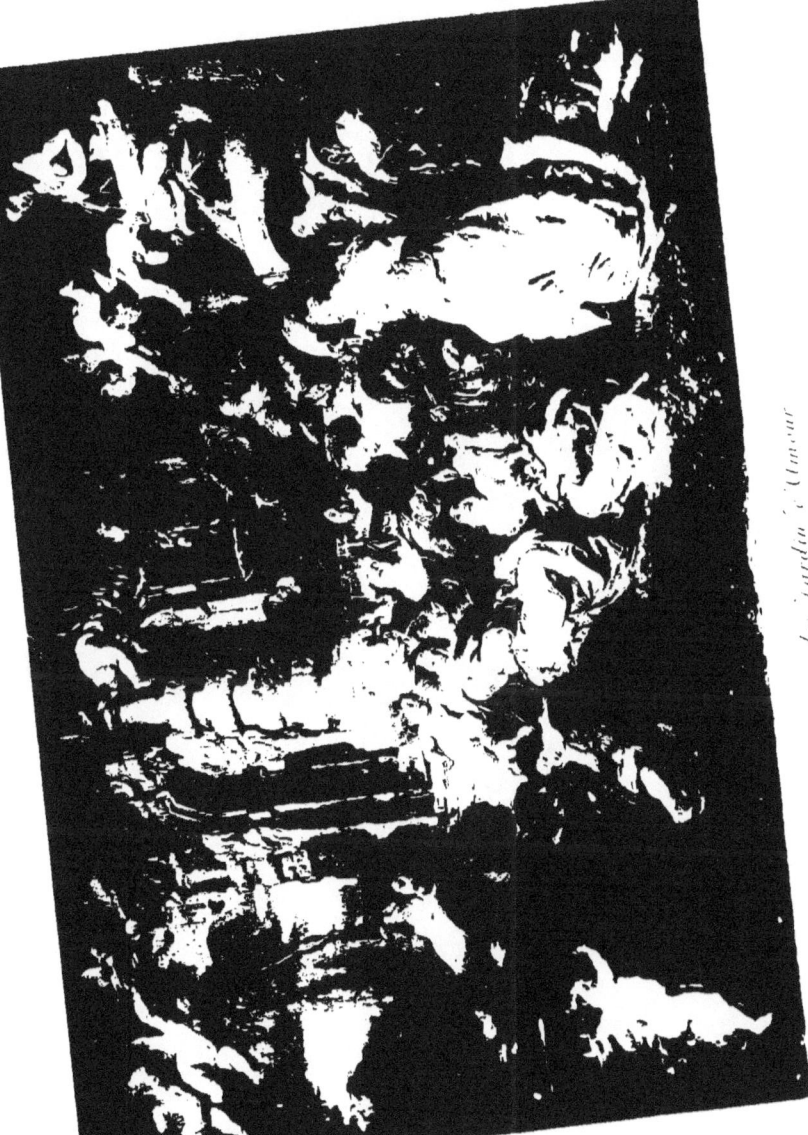

Le jardin d'Amour

Church, Antwerp. He personates St. George, while his two wives and other members of his family appear in the various characters of the picture. *Rubens at Sixty*, in the Vienna Museum, was painted about the same time as *St. George*, to which it bears a strong resemblance.

With a few notable exceptions, the best and most interesting of his works were done by Rubens after the year 1624. This period opens with the *Adoration of the Magi* (1624), in the Antwerp Museum, the *Resurrection of Lazarus* (1624), Berlin, and the *Assumption of the Virgin* (1626) in the Antwerp Cathedral. It includes the *Massacre of the Innocents (circa* 1635), Munich; *Christ carrying the Cross* (1635), Brussels Museum; the *Martyrdom of St. Liévin* (1635), Brussels; the *Venus* of Vienna (1630-1), and most of the pictures in our National Gallery. It ends with the *Virgin and Saints* (1639), in the chapel of the Rubens family, St. Jacques, Antwerp; with the *Three Graces* (1639), the *Jardin d'Amour* (1638), and other pictures at Madrid.

It is in 1624 that this third manner of painting begins to become evident, chiefly by the use of higher keys of colour, of shadows less marked, less heavy, less black or brown; of a thinner lay in, of pigment generally less dense; of tints more aerial, more fused and broken; of a touch slippery, expressive, and far more dexterous than that of the earlier periods. I think the change partly grew from the constant working over his pupils' painting which Rubens practised during the execution of the five large series of decorations which almost overlap each other from 1618 to 1623. He could not help thinking much of processes, of the economy of time and brushwork, of the use and quality of underpainting, of the value and importance of a few marked finishing touches. You may think, too, and I should agree with you, that, when he had brought the solid, heavy style of the second period to such perfection of process that it could be applied almost mechanically by his pupils to translate his sketches, Rubens would get sick of it as a method of working for himself, and that, using the experience he had acquired on the Luxembourg series, he would paint one or two large pictures entirely with his own hand as experiments in a new style. Such are the two canvases chosen by Max Rooses as marking the beginning of the third manner, namely, the *Adoration of the Magi*, Antwerp Museum, and the *Assumption of the Virgin*, Antwerp Cathedral.

One must not expect to perceive readily, or on any given occasion, the distinction between works painted before or after 1624. It has been said that Rubens gave indications of his later manner before 1624, and it should be added that in the later period he now and again reverted to a small style, a solid vehicle or a quiet and careful method of handling. Besides changes in Rubens one must take account also of the tastes of the spectator, the condition of the picture, and the accidents of exhibition at the time. It is useful to note the differences of opinion among those who really like and understand painting ; so much depends on the light in which the picture is seen, on its state as to dirt and varnish, and on the mind of the spectator at the particular moment, that even the same man holds different opinions on different occasions. Such transient influences combine with his permanent tastes and modify his judgment ; and perhaps nothing biasses him more strongly or more unconsciously than the character of what has previously occupied his mind and eye. Has he travelled through varied and exciting scenes, has he lived quietly in the study of nature, has he satiated his eye with indiscriminate and sensational picture-seeing, has he relaxed his taste with vapid eighteenth-century decoration, has he stimulated his faculties in the presence of some painter like Velazquez ? Whatever he has been taking in, the taste of it prepares his palate to receive with pleasure or disgust the art he is about to contemplate. Moreover, the painter, who thinks of his own art, who looks comparatively seldom at pictures, and then only at those he likes, naturally adopts a different attitude to art from that of the student of history whose pursuits lead him to examine with eagerness work of all kinds, of every degree of merit, and not seldom perhaps that of unsympathetic epochs.

Neither Delacroix nor Fromentin pretends to tell you the dates of all pictures by Rubens, to determine exactly the share that pupils took in their execution, or to assign every canvas to one of the accepted manners in which the artist painted. Painters never know so much about painting as critics and historians, or at any rate they affect to feel less confidence in their guesses. I have never heard any painter, even about his favourite artist, speak so cock-surely of " manners " and " attributions," as some writers will, even when they treat of quite obscure practitioners. It is true that painters have not hunted archives for confirmation of their suppositions ; it is true, however, that now and again they give way to

*Rubens at the age of Sixty. Imperial Gallery, Vienna.*
*From a Photograph by Löwy.*

an explosion of contemptuous certainty, as when Fromentin says of the
*Incredulity of St. Thomas* (Antwerp Museum), " Cela un Rubens ? quelle

erreur!" This only means, what every person will allow, that one finds nothing there of the qualities usually admired in a Rubens. Fromentin liked the *Adoration of the Magi* (St. Jean, Malines) better than any of the numerous versions. At any rate, he considered it the most serious; he called the celebrated canvas in the Antwerp Museum less carefully studied than that of Brussels, less accomplished than that of Malines. He speaks, however, with admiration of the audacity, certainty, and rapidity of the style of the Antwerp picture. It is, according to him, a "tour de force"; and he adds, "Pas un trou; pas une violence; une vaste demi-teinte claire et des lumières sans excès enveloppent toutes les figures appuyées l'une sur l'autre." With admiring zeal he also praises the sure, rapid, and surprising execution of other pictures, as the *Miraculous Draught of Fishes* (Notre Dame, Malines), the *Coup de Lance* (Antwerp Museum), the *Descent from the Cross*, and the *Elevation of the Cross* (Antwerp Cathedral). But the *Magi* at Malines he considers the final expression of its subject, and one of the finest efforts of Rubens in the spectacular kind of art. He prefers it to the *Miraculous Draught of Fishes*, although his interest in that astonishing canvas caused him to write much more fully upon it, and in his most witty and intelligent vein. The *Trinity*, the *Christ à la Paille*, the *St. Catharine*, and some others at Antwerp, Fromentin liked little better than he did the *Incredulity of St. Thomas*. The *Trinity* which Rooses dates 1620, Fromentin would assign to the pre-Italian period in spite of the foreshortening of Christ's body. The *Vierge au Perroquet*, "beau tableau presque impersonnel," smacks in his opinion of Italy and recalls Venice. Fromentin wonders why Van Dyck turned to it for inspiration. Although he admires the *Coup de Lance*, yet it is "un tableau décousu avec de grands vides, des aigreurs, de vastes taches un peu arbitraires, belles en soi, mais de rapports douteux." The *Education of the Virgin* is a charming decoration, but he would keep only the Virgin and the two winged figures. It is the *Communion of St. Francis* that he always comes back to in the Antwerp Museum. "Quand on a longuement examiné cette œuvre sans pareille, où Rubens se transfigure, on ne peut plus regarder rien, ni personne, ni les autres, ni Rubens lui-même; il faut pour aujourd'hui quitter le musée."

Only in a special study of the art of Rubens could I contrast with

*A Dance of Villagers. Museo del Prado, Madrid. From a Photograph by Braun, Clément, & Cie.*

those of Fromentin, the opinions of other men (not to speak of my own), which I have gathered together and compared in the course of reading or conversation. I will, however, touch upon the views of Eugène Delacroix, a painter who, in the late French revival of art, especially chose Rubens as an example, and a subject for study. Delacroix says : " At Antwerp, the *Communion of St. Francis*, which I did not like, has become my favourite ; and I also liked *Christ on the Knees of the Eternal Father (i.e.* the *Trinity*), which must be of the same time " (which is indeed of the following year). He agreed with Fromentin as to the splendid mastery of *Christ carrying the Cross* (1637), and the *Martyrdom of St. Liévin* (1635), at Brussels. Concerning the *Adorations of the Magi*, at first he liked best that of Brussels, but finally, he found it too dry and preferred the Antwerp picture. Unlike Fromentin, he could not tear himself away from the *Vierge au Perroquet* and the *Trinity* any more than from the *Communion of St. Francis*. Delacroix states that Rubens begins by modelling his figures in a thin half-tint, upon which he afterwards plants the strongest darks and highest lights, much after the manner in which Corot usually treated trees. He thinks that Rubens, unlike Veronese, often painted details in afterwards, such as the eyes, eyebrows, corners of the mouth, and worked them into the wet paint. In this account he describes the good works only, for the harder and inferior pictures, in his opinion, were painted bit by bit, separately.

It may be well to say that Rooses considers the *Trinity*, the *Education of the Virgin*, the *Vierge au Perroquet* at Antwerp, and the *Jesus, St. John, two Angels and a Lamb* at Berlin, in a large measure the work of pupils, and merely retouched by Rubens. He admits the tameness of the *Incredulity of St. Thomas*, but considers it entirely by the hand of the master. Neither Delacroix nor Fromentin ever saw, at least never spoke of, *Helen Fourment with a Fan* (1630-31, Hermitage), *Helen and Rubens in their Garden* (1630-31, Munich), the *Jardin d'Amour* (1638, Madrid), *Rubens at Sixty* (Vienna), or the *Dance of Peasants* (1639, Madrid). These Rooses praises as wholly by Rubens, and very precious examples of his different kinds of work. All but the last contain family portraits of great beauty and historical value. For my own part I admire without reserve the two Madrid canvases with their exquisite workmanship, their

G

wonderful movement and gesture, and their tender and delicious colouring. Yet I confess that from no picture by Rubens do I get such a
strong conviction of truth, such a sensation of natural life, and such an
illusion of the ugly or unfamiliar made beautiful as I do from the *Four
Heads of a Negro* (Brussels). I think that even the black and white
illustration to this monograph suffices to convey an impression of its
dignified truth.

# INDEX

THE END

*Printed by* R. & R. CLARK, LIMITED, *Edinburgh*